"Don't touch me!"
she cried desperately

If she said it often enough, she might believe it.

"Why the hell shouldn't I touch you?" he asked in a voice rough with emotion. "You're my wife, I want you."

"No...."

His eyes widened with dawning realization, dark, fevered. "Did you really think it all came for free?" he asked harshly. "With no price to pay? Your white body has haunted me for three years. You're mine—you've always been mine—but now it's legal. I can't believe you entered this marriage so naively."

"You hate me," she whispered, her heart clenching in pain.

Alex smiled, a rare tenderness glimmering in the depths of his eyes. "No, Talia, I don't hate you. I want you—as you want me."

PATRICIA LAKE

fated affair

Harlequin Books

TORONTO • NEW YORK • LONDON
AMSTERDAM • PARIS • SYDNEY • HAMBURG
STOCKHOLM • ATHENS • TOKYO • MILAN

Harlequin Presents first edition October 1983
ISBN 0-373-10634-3

Original hardcover edition published in 1983
by Mills & Boon Limited

CHAPTER ONE

TALIA felt a faint pang of sickness sliding in her stomach as she stepped off the bus. It had been a long journey and the bus had been very stuffy.

She took a deep calming breath and looked at her watch. She was a little early and she wished now that she had forced herself to eat something before leaving the flat.

She felt faint, a combination of nerves and hunger, the strain of the past months almost showing on her pale tense face, and for some reason she had the terrible irrational feeling that this was her last chance to get her life sorted out, to secure some sort of a future for Matty and herself. She couldn't afford to make a mess of this interview, as she had of others, she just couldn't, and the weight of that knowledge lay like a stone on her already overtaxed mind.

She walked briskly down the narrow country road. The sun beat down relentlessly. It was so hot today, the air very still, smelling of grass and flowers, a heat haze shimmering on the road.

It was also very quiet, the only evidence of the large houses she knew to be set back from the road being the tall, somehow intimidating gates she passed as she hunted for the house of her prospective—*she hoped* prospective employer.

Finding it all too soon, she glanced nervously at her watch again, smoothing back her shining auburn hair, checking the lines of her smart silk suit, her stomach suddenly churning.

She took another deep breath, desperately trying to

5

pull herself together, and pushing open the heavy wrought-iron gates, began walking quickly up the long drive until she reached the front door of the imposing stone house.

It was a beautiful house, making her wish all the more desperately that she could secure this job.

Yet another hurried glance at her wristwatch told her that she was exactly on time, so she pressed the bell and waited, able to hear her own heart beating in her ears. The door was flung open within minutes and Talia found herself facing a tall, finely-built, dark-haired young man, who she would have guessed was about seventeen years old.

Laughingly appraising blue eyes met hers. 'Hi, you must be Miss Montague.' His voice was friendly, curious, a soft American drawl. 'And right on time, too. Leon will appreciate that.'

Talia smiled, her nervousness easing a little at his open charm. 'Yes, I'm Talia Montague. I have an appointment with Mr Miller at two o'clock.'

The young man held out his hand, smiling back at her. 'I'm Jake, Leon's son. Come inside.'

They shook hands, his informality relaxing her. She liked him—a good omen. Jake showed her into a luxuriously furnished lounge. 'Would you like some coffee?'

Talia shook her head; she was too strung up to even think about a drink. All she wanted to do was to get the interview over and done with. 'No, thank you.'

The young man's blue eyes were suddenly under-standing. 'I'll go and tell Leon you're here. And don't worry, I have the feeling that everything is going to work out just fine.'

He disappeared before she had time to thank him for his kindness, his reassurance. She turned round and gazed blankly round the room, beautifully designed and decorated in pale blues and rich, dark reds. It was comfortable and informal and spoke of indolence, of wealth. If she could only get this job. . . .

'Leon will see you now. If you'll follow me, I'll show you to the study.' Jake had appeared behind her, his voice making her jump. She swung round, her smile stiff, her face uncertain. 'Of course . . . thank you.'

Jake stared at her, a certain gentleness in his face. 'Nervous?'

She nodded mutely.

'Don't be,' he told her firmly. 'I suspect that the job is already yours. Come on.' She had to smile as she followed him across the parquet floor of the high hall. If she only had his confidence, his carefree nonchalance!

They arrived in front of an arched wooden door. Jake knocked sharply and Talia heard the command to enter with a churning of her stomach.

'Good luck,' Jake smiled. 'And remember, his bark is worse than his bite.'

He opened the door for her and she stepped inside, finding herself in a large booklined room. The man behind the imposing mahogany desk rose to his feet as she entered, coming forward hand outstretched.

His eyes skimmed over her, lightning-fast, and she had the feeling that he had easily summed her up, discovered and assessed everything about her in those first few seconds.

'How do you do, Miss Montague. Won't you sit down?'

Talia murmured something polite, her smile bright and did as he suggested, declining his offer of a drink.

She watched him from beneath her lashes. Leon Miller was tall and well-built, with thick dark hair and a strong attractive face. In his early forties, he had a smile as easy and as charming as his son's, and Talia's fear disappeared, a certain liking for him springing up in her immediately, despite the edge of ruthlessness she could see in his face. And she had expected that anyway.

Leon Miller was a rich, successful American businessman. He would not have reached such a position of power without the quality of ruthlessness.

'I must confess, Miss Montague, you're a good deal younger than I expected, and to be perfectly honest, I'm looking for an older woman.' His voice broke into her reverie, the transatlantic drawl lazy and pronounced, belying the seriousness of his words.

'I can work as well as any older woman, Mr Miller, I can assure you.' Her earnest reply hid the sinking of her heart. It seemed his mind was already made up and the interview had barely begun. She could not allow herself the luxury of giving up without a fight.

'Do you know what the job involves?' His dark blue eyes pierced her through the haze of smoke from the cigar he lit, and his face gave nothing away.

'I understand from the agency that you have three children to be taken care of, and there would be general household duties——'

'A heavy demanding job, in fact,' Leon Miller cut in. 'Do you have any experience of such work?'

'I have experience with children and I believe I could run the house fairly easily,' she said, with a confidence she was far from feeling, her smile still radiantly bright. 'Yes, I'm sure I could do it, and I'd like you to give me a chance to prove myself.'

She knew she was being pushy, acting totally out of character, but she *needed* this job and she had no intention of letting it slip through her fingers because Leon Miller thought her young and incapable. She felt reckless with the knowledge that she had both everything and nothing to lose.

'How old are you, Miss Montague?' Those dark blue eyes had never left her face, assessing, curious. She considered lying for a second, then dismissed the idea. 'Twenty-two,' she replied simply; and when she saw the slight raising of his eyebrows added, 'But I don't think that automatically disqualifies me for the job, in fact it would probably be an advantage where the children are concerned.' She watched him with bated breath as he stubbed out his cigar. Had she gone too far? Her dark eyes were unconsciously pleading and very beautiful as she stared at him, *willing* him to give her a chance.

'Why is this job so important to you?'

She could have imagined it, but she was sure she saw a slight softening in those steely blue eyes, in the uncompromising line of his mouth.

'Jobs are not easy to come by,' she said lightly, hoping as soon as she said it that her voice wasn't too light, too obvious.

'Which doesn't answer my question,' Leon Miller said, just as lightly. Talia was silent for a second or two, trying to decide whether or not to tell him about Matty. If she got the job, and the possibility seemed more remote as the interview wore on, she would have to tell him anyway, and if she didn't, although it didn't bear thinking about, she realised now that she had nothing to lose.

'The truth is that I have a young son and I need the accommodation this job offers,' she finally replied, her body stiffening with a strangely innocent dignity. Leon Miller stared at her.

'And your husband? Are you divorced?'

'I'm not married,' she said quietly, thinking that it was probably time to leave.

'I think you should tell me a little about yourself,' he suggested quite gently, lighting another cigar.

'It's quite a catalogue of woes,' she warned with a slight smile, very surprised that he was willing to carry on with the interview. Experience had taught her that to mention the fact that she was an unmarried mother at an interview was disastrous.

'If it's a long story, perhaps it's time we had that coffee.' Amazingly he was smiling too.

'Thank you, I'd like that.' Hope burned in her eyes. Did she have a chance?

Five minutes later Jake appeared, balancing a tray in one hand. He smiled broadly at Talia as he set the tray down on the desk, and seemed about to speak, but one look at his father sent him silently from the room.

'Jake seems quite taken with you,' Leon Miller remarked, as he poured coffee for them both.

Talia felt a little flustered, unsure of what to say. 'We seemed to hit it off right away.' She sipped her coffee nervously, aware that for some incredible reason she *did* have a chance, and praying that she wouldn't say anything too stupid.

'You're the only one so far,' he informed her laughingly. 'He seems to have taken a positive dislike to all the other applicants I've seen.'

Talia smiled and said nothing, her feeling of hopefulness growing by the second.

'What is your son's name?' Leon Miller suddenly asked.

'Matty.' Talia's face was proud with love, gentle, as she thought of the little boy.

'And how old is he?'

'Nearly three years old.'

'Forgive me for prying, but Matty's father?'

'He doesn't know Matty exists,' Talia cut in flatly. 'A situation that suits me perfectly.' She bit her lip, not wanting to think about Alex, not now, not when she was concentrating so hard on getting this job.

'I'm sorry,' Leon Miller smiled charmingly, 'I didn't mean to upset you.'

'No, I'm sorry, I hope I wasn't rude. It's just that I prefer not to think about the time I spent with ... with Matty's father.' She was candidly honest.

'I understand. Where are you living at the moment? And what about previous jobs, you said you had experience with children?'

Talia sighed expressively at the questions. 'It's a long story.'

'Start from the beginning,' he suggested with a smile.

'Well, before I had Matty I was working for an advertising agency—a secretarial post. Obviously, I had to give up my job there when he was born, and I had nowhere to go because I had to give up my flat as well.'

'What about your parents? Couldn't they have supported you until you found something?'

She heard the shocked curiosity in his voice and explained, 'My mother died when I was seventeen. I was living in London at the time, I'd grown away from my parents very young. My father married again almost immediately and moved to New Zealand. We'd never been very close; I think he always resented the way I tied him down. Anyway, I never hear from him now, except at Christmas and birthdays.' There was no trace of self-pity in her voice. Her father was, and always had been a stranger to her. During her childhood he had seemed remote, detached from Talia and her mother. A merchant seaman by trade, he had been away for long periods of time, so she had hardly missed him when he emigrated, although it had been quite a blow to find herself so alone.

He had written, of course, offering her a home with

him and his new wife, but Talia had suspected that the invitation was prompted by guilt and a long-standing sense of duty. He had made a new life for himself and she had been unsure of a genuine welcome. And she had been content with her job, her flat, her life in London, and soon after had met Alex. . . .

She snapped her thoughts back to the present, using all her willpower to push from her mind the image of that strong, powerfully-attractive face, that hard sensual mouth, those cool grey eyes. Damn him, she would *not* think of him.

'So, what did you do?' Leon Miller prompted gently.

'Well, unfortunately one of the conditions of my lease on the flat categorically stated no children, and obviously I couldn't hide the fact that I was pregnant, but luckily a friend of a friend who lived in France was looking for a nanny for her children, and that's what I've been doing for the past two years.' She grimaced ruefully. 'Now, though, she and her husband are getting a divorce. She's moving into a smaller house and she'll be looking after the children herself. She'll have neither the room nor the money to keep me on. So I'm out of work, I'm staying with a friend at the moment, but as you can imagine, it's not very satisfactory. She only has a tiny flat and I feel terrible about putting her to so much trouble.' She broke off, smilingly wryly. 'Sounds dreadful, doesn't it, like something out of a Dickens novel. You can't say I didn't warn you, though.'

She had easily glossed over the terrible time she'd had. The worst time of her life had been when she was carrying Matty. Alex had gone for ever and she had been homeless, jobless and very nearly penniless. She shuddered even now when she thought about it.

'It really wasn't as awful as it sounds,' she lied with

a faintly embarrassed smile. 'And it certainly taught me how to stand on my own two feet, which can't be bad.'

Leon Miller smiled, his blue eyes genuinely amused. 'I'm sure you're understating the case, and I admire your strength.'

Talia shrugged, her dark eyes guarded yet bright. 'Now that you know the whole sordid story, Mr Miller, can you tell me whether or not I still have a chance of getting this job?' She was charmingly blunt, and very surprised with herself. She had told him so much. She had never opened up so easily to a stranger before. Being an unmarried mother with a small child, she had learned to guard her privacy jealously. There were too many people still ready to condemn without caring about or knowing the facts.

And yet she had practically given Leon Miller her life story within half an hour of meeting him.

There was something about him that inspired confession and honesty, though now she was a little afraid that she had told him too much. She felt embarrassed.

She looked into his face and wondered why she had revealed so much, so easily. It had never happened before at an interview. Never. Usually she was reluctant to divulge even the smallest piece of information about her private life.

Perhaps I'm more desperate than I realise, she thought with a sigh. I need this job and perhaps I've deliberately made my life seem dreadful, hoping that he will take pity on me.

Leon Miller was smoking, watching her through narrowed eyes. Suddenly he smiled, decision reached.

'The job is yours, Miss Montague, for a three-month trial period. If everything works out during that time, you'll be taken on permanently.'

Talia stared at him, open-mouthed, hardly able to believe her ears or her luck. 'Really?' she asked inanely.

'Yes, really,' he smiled.

'Are you taking me on because you feel sorry for me? What I said about my life——'

'I'm hiring you because you can do the job,' he cut in firmly. 'Because you've been honest, because I like you, because my son also likes you, and because I need somebody as soon as possible. Okay?'

'Okay,' Talia smiled, having to restrain herself from leaping off her chair and hugging him. The strain of the past weeks fell away, leaving her almost lightheaded, and she had to concentrate and listen as he began talking again.

The salary seemed enormous and she agreed to it immediately.

'You'll have your own rooms, of course, but you will live with the family. Jake you've already met, he's the eldest. Then there's Belle, she's ten, and Vinnie, six. The cooking and the heavy cleaning is all taken care of by Mrs Rodale, so you don't have to worry about that,' he told her with brisk efficiency. 'My business means that I have to travel a great deal, that's one of the reasons I need somebody here, looking after the children——'

They both heard the telltale noise outside the study door. 'Jake, come in here.' There was laughter in his voice. The door opened slowly and Jake appeared, a crooked smile turning up the corners of his mouth.

'Obviously I don't have to tell you the good news.' Leon Miller smiled at his son, who was staring at Talia.

'You've got the job?'

She nodded. 'Yes, I've got the job.'

'Great! When will you be starting?'

Talia turned to Leon Miller, her dark eyes questioning.

'As soon as possible,' he told her crisply. 'Would the end of this week suit you?'

She only had a few things to pack. It wouldn't take long at all. 'The end of this week would be fine.'

'Good. By the way, what's your Christian name? I can't keep calling you Miss Montague.'

'Talia,' she supplied with a smile.

'Okay, Talia, you'd better call me Leon. We don't stand on formality here.'

The next hour flashed by in a whirl. Talia was introduced to Mrs Rodale, a thin, kindly-looking woman, and they chatted over coffee before she was shown over the house. It was beautiful, spacious and very luxurious, her own rooms bright and airy with more than enough room for Matty and herself.

She did not meet Vinnie or Belle. Vinnie was staying with a friend, she was told by Jake, and Belle was at her ballet lesson.

On hearing that she had travelled to the house on the bus, Leon insisted on driving her back to Kate's flat. He also promised to send a car for her the day she moved in.

Talia sat in the front of the enormous car, in a happy daze as they sped towards the city. There was a haze of dreamlike unreality over the afternoon's events and she half expected to wake up at any moment and find herself jobless again. When she looked back on the interview it all seemed as though it had been easy. The job was hers, and she and Matty had a future again.

Kate was waiting by the front door of the flat when Talia arrived. 'How did it go?' she demanded immediately. 'Was that Leon Miller in that incredible car I saw you pulling up in? What happened? What's he like?'

Talia laughed, unable to get a word in edgeways, and just waited until her friend paused for breath.

'Yes, it was Leon Miller and yes, I have got the job. I start at the end of the week.'

The two girls hugged each other and danced into the flat. Matty was sitting on the floor, playing with a plastic train. His clear grey eyes lit up as he saw his mother, and his sweet childish mouth split into a huge grin, soon to disappear as concentration on his toys returned.

Talia kissed his soft cheek before accepting the cup of tea Kate handed to her and lighting a cigarette.

They sat down at the table near the window and for the first time in hours, Talia allowed herself to relax.

'Tell me all about it,' Kate pressed eagerly.

'The house is beautiful,' Talia told her. 'But I was convinced I hadn't got the job. As soon as I met him he told me that he was looking for somebody older. I ended up telling him about Matty because I could see the job slipping away from me, and amazingly, after that, everything went fine.' She shook her head, incredulity in every line of her face. 'I can hardly believe it.'

Kate smiled, her black curls glinting in the heavy sunlight. 'I'm so glad for you. I've been quite worried these past few weeks, I can tell you. And now everything has worked out. You've been so pale and tense, I could hardly bear it.'

'Oh, Kate, you shouldn't have worried. Something was bound to turn up—and now it has,' Talia laughed, touched that Kate cared enough to have been worrying about her. They had been friends since schooldays, years before, both the same age. Kate was tall and very slender with a forceful, vibrant personality. She was separated from her husband—they had married too young, she always said—and had recently given up her

job to work on a book. She had offered Talia and
Matty accommodation for as long as they needed it,
when Talia's job as a nanny had ended, and because
she worked at home, she was more than willing to look
after Matty while Talia searched for a job. But the flat
was small and Talia knew that Kate needed peace and
quiet to write. She was overwhelmed by Kate's
kindness, and the only way she could repay that
kindness was by moving out as soon as she could,
hence part of her desperation for a job.

'I know what we'll do,' Kate said suddenly. 'We'll
celebrate. We'll go out for a meal tonight. My mum
will babysit, and you need a night out—you haven't
been out for ages, and this is a perfect opportunity.'

Talia nodded, excited by the prospect. It was true,
she hadn't been out for weeks; not only had she been
too worried about the future to enjoy herself, but she
had needed to conserve the small amount of money
she had, just in case nothing turned up.

'On one condition,' she agreed. 'I pay for the meal.
I want to say thanks for all you've done for us.'

Kate laughed, obviously pleased. 'I accept,' she said
gracefully.

So, with Matty safely sleeping in his bed and Kate's
mother, a retired nurse, due to arrive in twenty
minutes, Talia took a shower, then dressed in a black
silk dress, making up her face and brushing out her
shining auburn hair, leaving it to hang loose around
the fragile bones of her face. Without conceit, she
knew that she looked good, her body perfectly curved
and seductive in the black silk, her face delicate, pale,
her mouth wide and gentle.

They took a taxi towards the river; the restaurant
they chose was near the Houses of Parliament. They
sipped drinks in the bar and Talia told Kate all about
the interview again.

'Lucky you,' said Kate, half wistfully. 'Leon Miller looks quite a man.'

'Yes, he's very attractive. I've been wondering about his wife, though.'

'Don't you ever read the papers?' Kate asked incredulously. 'It was in all the gossip columns a couple of weeks ago.'

'What was?' Talia had no idea what her friend was talking about.

'Alicia Miller. Doesn't the name ring a bell?'

Talia frowned, then remembered. 'The model? *She's* Leon Miller's wife?'

Kate nodded, her expression one of patient exasperation. 'The very same. Apparently she's in Rome with that young singer. The scandal has been raging for weeks now—you can be *dim* sometimes!'

'I didn't connect them at all,' Talia said absently. 'I had no idea. How awful for the children, having to live with all that.'

'Lucky for them they'll have you to look after them,' Kate said gently.

Talia smiled at the compliment, still thinking about Alicia Miller. She was known world-wide, very much in demand. There had been rumours of her affair with a young rock singer for weeks before she had finally jetted off to Rome with him. It was hard for Talia to connect the photographs she had seen of the stunningly beautiful Alicia Miller with the house she had been interviewed at that afternoon. Talia could not imagine her living there with Leon and the children.

Alicia Miller was glossy, remote, almost unreal; it was practically impossible to connect her with ordinary, everyday life.

The restaurant was softly lit and they were shown to their table by a dark-skinned deferential waiter, who handed them enormous leather-bound menus.

Over the meal they chatted about Kate's book and Talia's plans for leaving the flat. The food was delicious, perfectly prepared and served. Over coffee, Talia was laughing at something Kate had said, pushing the silky weight of her hair behind her ears, when she noticed the man being shown to the table opposite to theirs.

As she realised who she was absently staring at, she froze as though struck dead. It was Alex Jordan, Matty's father, the only man she had ever loved, the only man she had ever hated!

Her heart stopped beating for one awful moment, her fingers tightening unbearably around the fragile china coffee cup, the smile and the laughter dying on her lips.

She had not seen him for three years, had not wanted to see him, and now he was seated only a couple of yards away from her and she couldn't drag her eyes away. He was alone, although she noticed that the table was set for three. He had not changed at all and she would have noticed the slightest change, she knew his face so well. Thick dark hair brushed back from a hard boned serious face, a beautifully moulded mouth, warm, sensual and disturbing grey eyes that could flash silver with ice or melt darkly with sleepy passion. He wore his power and wealth with sophisticated ease. Talia's heart was beating again, too fast now, deafening her. She slowly put down her coffee cup, her eyes still on Alex Jordan, wide, fearful. She felt physically sick with the realisation that every time she looked at Matty she was looking at Alex. The resemblance was disturbing, frightening. She felt the colour pouring back into her face, but still she could not drag her eyes away from him. Why did he have to be here, tonight of all nights? Her pleasure at getting the job, at the enjoyable evening spent with Kate, at the delicious food, all abruptly disappeared as she gazed at that proud dark head. She felt only anger and bitterness and hatred.

And as though sensing the desperate intensity of her gaze, he suddenly turned his head slightly and those cool grey eyes met hers, totally blank for a split second, then darkening with recognition. There was no other acknowledgement between them. They stared at each other, unable to look away. Talia felt a cramping in her stomach like a physical blow, the contact between them electric, but could read nothing in the cool grey depths; they were totally blank, almost like a mirror.

'Talia, what is it?' Kate was staring at her worriedly, noticing the pale rigid shock on her friend's face. Talia was unable to say a word, her mouth was dry, her throat blocked.

'Talia!' Kate's voice was higher, more concerned now. 'Are you ill?'

Talia managed to shake her head, tearing her eyes away from Alex Jordan, her whole body stiff with fear and shock, her eyes noting the woman who had just approached his table.

Alex was moving to his feet, smiling, taking her hand and raising it to his lips. The woman was slim and elegant, approaching sixty, Talia would have guessed, although she had once been very beautiful; her clothes were obviously expensive, her grey hair dramatically streaked with white. Talia would have been curious if she hadn't been so desperately shocked.

'I want . . . I want to leave,' she managed through numb lips.

'What is it?' Kate was frowning.

'Alex Jordan.' Talia stumbled betrayingly over the name.

'*What? In here?*'

'Sitting behind you.' Talia swallowed convulsively and got shakily to her feet. She would not, *could not* stay, and she didn't give a damn what connotations he put on her practically running from the restaurant. She just wanted to get away.

'I'm sorry, Kate, I have to go.'

'Wait a second, I'll come with you.' Kate grabbed her handbag and stood up, surreptitiously glancing at the man seated behind her.

Talia was already walking away, knowing that Alex was watching her, feeling the blank probe of his eyes on her body as she almost ran from his view.

Kate paid the bill, collected Talia's coat and organised a taxi to take them back to the flat. Talia was numb, silent, her eyes blind, her mind in total chaos as she sat inside the darkness of the taxi. Kate offered her a cigarette. She accepted it with trembling fingers.

'Are you all right, Talia?' She focused her eyes on Kate, pulling herself together as she saw her friend's worried concern.

'Yes.' Her voice was husky, disturbed. 'It was the shock, that's all . . . seeing him after all this time. . . .' Her face burned with a flaring of colour. 'I shouldn't have run away. . . . I made a fool of myself and I spoilt your meal, but I couldn't stay there. I'm sorry, Kate.'

'Don't apologise, we'd finished anyway,' her friend said reassuringly, truthfully.

Talia could tell that she was curious. She had never told Kate or anybody else the whole story about Alex and herself. It was too painful, too private. Kate knew, of course, that Alex was Matty's father—that had been too obvious to hide from someone who had met Alex. She also knew that the affair between Talia and Alex was long over, but she knew none of the details.

Her own behaviour in the restaurant this evening had given a lot away, Talia realised, and Kate's imagination was probably running riot.

A thought struck her. 'Kate, I don't want Alex to know *anything* at all about Matty—not now or ever. Promise me you'll never say anything, you'll never tell him,' she begged, leaning forward. Her eyes were wide, very desperate, beseeching. She was hardly aware of what she was saying, her ravaged emotions totally in control of everything she was saying and doing.

'Promise me,' she repeated again.

Kate was frowning. 'You mean Alex doesn't know?' Her voice was incredulous, her face shocked.

'No, Alex doesn't know. I don't want him to know.'

'Talia, don't you think——?'

'Alex gave up any rights to Matty years ago, even before Matty was born,' Talia said coldly. 'He mustn't find out.' There was a fragile edge of hysteria behind the icy statement, and Kate responded to it.

'Don't worry, I won't tell him a thing,' she promised very clearly.

Talia's body seemed to sag with relief. 'Thanks.' It was all she could manage, the crazy events of the day were catching up with her. She was drained, an empty shell and by the time they reached the flat, she had only enough energy to look in on Matty before literally falling into bed exhausted, Alex's hard face haunting her as she dropped into a light, uneasy sleep.

CHAPTER TWO

SHE started packing away both Matty's clothes and her own the next day, but as she worked her thoughts were filled with Alex Jordan. Seeing him the night before had been a terrible shock and had brought back memories she had hoped long forgotten.

Taking a break for a cup of coffee and a cigarette, she watched Matty playing. He was singing to himself, his small brow furrowed with concentration.

She would be glad to be working again, and it would be good for Matty to have the company of other children and the run of the vast gardens at Leon Miller's house.

She could hear Kate's typewriter from the bedroom. It would be good for Kate as well. She would be able to work in peace.

I should be happy that everything is finally working out so well, she told herself. Instead she felt tired, lethargic and very depressed.

Later in the afternoon, she took Matty to the park to play. He needed the fresh air and the freedom to run about, and it gave Kate a break as well. They sat on the grass in the warm sunshine. Matty was watching another little boy, about the same age as himself, who was playing ball with his father.

He turned to Talia. 'That little boy's got a daddy.'

'Yes, darling.' Talia smiled at him, pushing a wayward lock of dark hair from his eyes.

'Why don't I got a daddy? Jenny and Paul got one.'

She felt inadequacy rushing over her at his childish words. What could she say to him? His clear grey eyes stared into hers as he waited for his answer.

'Not all children have daddies,' she said at last.

It was not good enough, and Matty frowned, about to ask more questions, until she diverted him by offering to buy him an icecream. It was a mean trick, she thought ruefully, but he was too young to understand that his father didn't care, didn't even know of his existence.

Questions about his father were coming more and more frequently as he grew older. Sooner or later she would have to tell him the truth. It was a problem she constantly pushed to the back of her mind, constantly worried about and dreaded.

Would Matty seek Alex out when he was old enough? She tried unsuccessfully to halt her thoughts straying back to Alex.

It had been a coincidence seeing him last night. It meant nothing and she wouldn't see him again. A small voice in her head reminded her, as she was telling herself this so fiercely, that there was nothing coincidental about Alex Jordan. He took what he wanted and coincidence played no part in his life.

As though it was yesterday she could remember the day she first met him.

She had been typing away at her desk when he had arrived to see Mark Fitzgerald, her boss. It was no secret around the building that Alex Jordan had recently become one of the agency's biggest clients, and Mark was ecstatic about it.

Talia, concentrating hard on her work, trying to clear up a backlog, did not even notice him arriving, until she happened to glance up to find him just closing the door of the outer office.

She recognised him immediately, of course, but was unprepared for the shock of trembling awareness that ran through her as his cool grey eyes met hers.

'Hello,' he smiled, and she felt the muscles in her stomach tightening. 'Is Mark in?' His eyes were appraising as he waited for her answer, lingering on her shining hair and vulnerable mouth.

'He isn't in the office at the moment, Mr Jordan, but I'm expecting him back at any second.' Her voice was husky and she had to fight to keep it even. What was the matter with her?

'I'll wait,' he said, and smiled slightly as she flushed.

She watched from beneath her lashes as he coiled his powerful body into one of the comfortable leather chairs opposite her desk. He was taller than she had imagined him to be, well over six foot, and the hard muscled strength of his body could not be hidden beneath the expensive tailoring of his suit.

She tried to concentrate on her work, ignoring him, but that was impossible. Her fingers flew over the typewriter keys, making more mistakes than a beginner, and for some crazy reason her heart was beating very fast, drumming in her ears.

'Do you mind if I smoke?' His question made her jump and hectic colour ran up her small face as she looked at him again.

'Not at all. Could I get you some coffee?' She should have asked him before.

He shook his head. 'No, thanks.'

She lowered her head immediately, yet could not help herself watching him covertly as he placed a thin cheroot between his lips.

She stared at his hands, tanned, very strong, then at his face, hard-jawed, angled, shadowed beneath the high cheekbones. He was compellingly, devastatingly attractive. His cool grey eyes held awareness, wisdom and a masculine sexuality that drew Talia like a magnet.

Their eyes met again, his narrowed, curious, and she looked away, feeling flustered and unable to cope, because no man had ever had such an effect on her before. Fool, she chastised herself fiercely, pull yourself together!

She knew all about him, of course; everybody did. He was fabulously wealthy, owning more companies than Talia had had hot dinners. He worked hard, so she'd heard, and he played hard. Beautiful, successful women fell at his feet, that was a matter of well documented fact, and now she had seen him face to face, she knew why.

'What's your name?' His voice was low, attractive, and her head jerked up.

'Talia Montague,' she heard herself replying in a thin high voice.

Alex Jordan stood up and walked indolently towards her desk, watching her, watching the restless shifting of her innocent dark eyes, the faint colour in her cheeks. He sat down on the edge of her desk, one leg idly swinging.

Talia kept her head down, her heart pounding, shivering as he reached out and tilted up her chin. He was smiling, an easy charming smile.

'You're beautiful,' he said softly. 'Very beautiful. Do you know that, Talia Montague?'

'I know that you're making fun of me,' she said quietly, her brown eyes hurt, confused.

Alex Jordan shook his head, the bright overhead light glinting in the darkness of his hair. 'Why should I do that?'

'Because you're waiting for Mark and you have nothing else to do,' she retorted tremulously, every nerve in her body responding to the strangely gentle touch of his long fingers on her jaw.

'Believe me, I'm not making fun of you.' His grey

eyes held hers, serious, very clear. 'You are beautiful.'
Then he smiled. 'Will you have dinner with me
tonight?'

Talia's eyes widened slightly, believing she must
have misheard him. Had Alex Jordan *really* asked her
out for dinner?

'Are you busy tonight?' he asked when she was
silent.

'N-No, but . . . but why are you asking me?' As
soon as she spoke, she wished she hadn't. He would
think her so stupid.

'Because I'd like to spend some time with you,' he
said calmly.

'I don't understand . . . you could ask anybody. . . .'
She faltered. Oh God, she was making such a terrible
fool of herself!

'I'm asking you,' he mocked gently. Talia stared at
him. She wanted to accept, more than anything, she
wanted to accept. She smiled, her face suddenly
radiant, unaware that Alex was still and staring,
caught by the beauty of that smile.

'Thank you, I'd like to have dinner with you
tonight,' she murmured politely.

So it had been arranged, and they had chatted
together, Alex making her laugh, easing her nervousness of him, until Mark arrived back from the
emergency meeting upstairs, apologising profusely to
Alex as they disappeared into his office. Talia had
been left alone with her work, breathless, stunned and
very happy.

Now, of course, she could see how stupid she had
been, accepting that invitation. She should have run
a mile when she heard those husky compliments.
Even at eighteen, she should not have been so
ridiculously naïve. How could she have thought that
a man like Alex Jordan could be seriously interested

in her? Even at that first meeting it had been too late. . . .

She shivered, even though the sun was so hot, and turned her full attention back to Matty, who had finished his icecream and was looking fractious and tired.

She sat him in his pushchair and walked slowly back to the flat, the loneliness that had been haunting her all morning crowding into her mind like a black cloud, blotting out everything else.

Kate was already preparing dinner when they got back. After giving Matty his supper, bathing him and putting him to bed, Talia set the table and helped with the meal. Kate seemed quiet, preoccupied, but Talia assumed she was thinking about her book until, over coffee, she suddenly said, 'Alex Jordan rang when you were at the park with Matty.'

Talia's stomach turned over. Oh God, she thought in panic, what on earth does he want?

'To speak to me?' she asked fairly calmly.

'Who else?'

'How did he know I was staying with you?' She had seen him for the first time in three years the night before, and already he knew where she lived.

Kate's shoulders lifted. 'I don't know, but he did.' She looked worried.

'What did you say to him?' Talia's sense of panic was growing by the second.

'I told him you were out and asked if he would like to leave a message. He said he'd ring back.'

Talia rested her head in her hands. She could not think why Alex should want to speak to her. He had made it very clear three years ago that it was all over between them. Unless he knew about Matty. . . .

She swallowed convulsively. 'You . . . you didn't mention Matty?'

'Of course not, I promised I wouldn't.' Kate poured more coffee for them both.

'I can't imagine what he wants,' Talia said quietly. 'We have absolutely nothing to say to each other.' She shook her head. 'I hate to ask you, Kate, but would you do me a favour? If he rings again, will you tell him I'm not here? Oh, and don't give him Leon Miller's address.'

'Okay,' Kate agreed calmly. She paused, then said, 'Look, I know it's none of my business, so you can tell me to shut up if you want, but last night, you were very upset, so did you mean what you said—that Alex knows nothing about Matty?'

Talia sipped her coffee, thinking hard, knowing that she owed Kate some sort of explanation. 'Alex made it very clear that it was all over between us, before I had a chance to tell him that I was pregnant. He didn't want to know, and by that time I'd found out . . . well, I'd found out things about him that. . . . Let's just say I didn't trust him any more, I didn't want to see him. I don't want him to know about Matty—he has no rights, no claim, on him. When Matty is older I'll explain everything to him and if he wants to see his father then obviously I'll let him. But right now Alex has the power to take Matty away from me, I know that, and I couldn't bear to lose him, he means everything to me.' Her eyes filled with tears. 'I know Matty needs a father and I don't know if I'm doing the right thing for him . . . but I do know that Alex means trouble. You do understand?'

Kate sighed, touching Talia's hand. 'Of course I understand. I'm sorry I interfered, and I won't tell him anything, I promise.'

Talia sniffed, feeling foolish, and managed a weak smile. 'I'll make some more coffee, shall I? I want something to do to take my mind off Alex.'

The telephone rang some hours later while they were watching television. Seated nearest to the phone, Talia automatically stretched out a hand to pick up the receiver, then froze, her heart beginning to pound. She silently passed the telephone to Kate, feeling ridiculous. She couldn't even answer the telephone!

'Hello?'

Talia listened, her hands playing nervously in her lap.

'No, I'm sorry, Talia isn't here.' Kate sounded calm, unruffled. 'Alex——' She shrugged her shoulders as she replaced the receiver. 'He hung up,' she explained with a grimace. 'And I'm sure he knew I was lying.'

Talia lit a cigarette, her hands trembling. 'Was he angry?' she asked carefully.

'He certainly was, but what could he do?'

'Why does he want to speak to me anyway?' Talia wondered aloud for the umpteenth time.

Kate shrugged again. 'I don't know, but he's a very determined man and if he wants to see you, I think he'll find a way.'

Talia sighed. 'I suppose I know that really. I'm just running away, putting off the moment—stupid, when I know how useless it is.'

Alex was determined, hard and forceful; he always got what he wanted. Always. If he wanted to see her, she would have to face him sooner or later. Putting him off would only make him more determined; she knew that for sure. But she needed a little time to prepare herself. Three years was a long time and she also had Matty to think about, and despite her terrible confusion, one thought remained clear. Alex must not find out about him.

She went to bed soon after, still very disturbed and worried, yet again unable to sleep, and by the following morning the persistent lack of rest was taking its toll, her skin paler than ever, bruised circles around her eyes, her temper short, irritable.

Catching her mood, Matty was unusually awkward and sullen over breakfast, and by midday Talia's nerves were at breaking point and she felt thoroughly exhausted.

Kate arrived back from the city and a business meeting about one, took one look at Talia and immediately took charge of Matty.

'I'll look after him for the afternoon,' she said firmly. 'Why don't you go for a walk? It'll clear your head and calm you down.'

Talia smiled gratefully. 'Thanks, I think I will. I don't know what I'd do without you, I really don't.'

It was another hot day, so she changed into jeans and a sleeveless cotton blouse, then strolled towards the park, enjoying the warmth of the sun on her face, the freedom of a little time alone, and as she walked she could feel some of the tension inside her draining away, her taut muscles slowly relaxing.

She was thinking hard, trying to clear her mind of the confusion that held her in its grip, and consequently did not notice the low black car pulling up in front of her, or the tall powerful figure of a man sliding from the driving seat, walking round to lean indolently against the hood, his arms folded across his chest, blocking her path.

As she arrived in front of him, her head lifted and she stopped dead in her tracks, her eyes widening.

'Hello, Talia,' Alex Jordan greeted her coolly, his narrowed eyes sliding over her in slow appraisal. 'Face to face at last!'

She did not mistake the mockery in his low voice, his knowledge that Kate had been lying on the telephone.

She could feel her heart racing, her mouth drying up. She could not say a word. She looked up at him in fearful silence, her eyes skittering over his wide shoulders, lean hips, the tight jeans that did not hide the strength of his legs.

Three years had left no mark on him at all. She forced herself to look into his dark face, desperately trying to gather her shattered composure, unable to read any expression in the grey eyes that held hers.

'Nothing to say?' he queried mockingly, making her feel foolish.

'Why should I have anything to say to you?' she asked coldly, finding her tongue at last, *hating* him because he could still affect every nerve in her body, even after all this time, even though she knew what kind of a man he was. She glanced round, furtively looking for escape.

Alex easily read her desperation and smiled slightly. 'You're not going anywhere,' he stated with softly spoken conviction. 'Not until we've talked.'

'*Talked?*' Talia was incredulous. 'What the hell do we have to talk about?'

Alex laughed, though the eyes that held hers were cold, blank. 'Three years is a long time, Talia, my love. I imagine we have plenty to talk about—old times being a good starting point.'

'I don't know how you dare——' she began heatedly, then bit back her angry words.

There was absolutely no point in arguing with him or trying to match his cynicism. He could use words like deadly weapons. Irrelevantly, something Mark had once said crept into her mind. 'Alex Jordan can kill with that tongue of his, so you'd better watch out, my darling. I'll bet he doesn't even spare sweet little innocents like you.' Strange how she remembered that, and how true, she thought bitterly. She couldn't say she hadn't been warned.

'How I dare to do what?' That mocking smile was pulling at his hard mouth again and Talia itched to slap it from existence.

'Just leave me alone!' she snapped, and turned away, intending to run if she had to, blinded by her hatred of him.

'Oh no, you don't!' He caught her arm, his fingers curling around her slender elbow, not hurting her but not hiding the immense strength of his grasp, warning her not to struggle.

'Let me go!' Her plea was breathless, panic-stricken, the light touch of his fingers shooting fire along her arm, weakening her knees.

'For God's sake don't be so childish,' Alex bit out coldly, not making any move to release her. 'I have no intention of abducting you.'

'Then what *do* you want?' she demanded unsteadily, trying to control her fearful panic.

'Have you eaten?'

The question was totally unexpected and he was actually smiling.

Confused, Talia answered honestly, 'No, I haven't, why?'

'We could have lunch together,' he suggested, his quiet tone not quite concealing the faint edge of warning behind the words.

'You've got to be joking!' His audacity took her so completely by surprise that she was careless in reply and immediately regretted it, realising how she had angered him.

'I can assure you I'm not.' His mouth tightened ominously, his grip on her bare arm hurting her now. She tried unsuccessfully to pry his fingers away, angry at his strength. 'Take your hands off me!' she hissed, uncaring that they were standing in the middle of the pavement on a fairly busy road, their argument open to anybody caring to listen. 'I wouldn't have lunch with you if you were the last man on earth!'

Alex clucked his tongue, his mouth still smiling even though she knew that he was very angry, that her insult had hit home.

'What an impolite, bitter child you are,' he mused infuriatingly.

'What do you expect?' she flung at him, hurt by his cold mockery, angry because she could feel the tears stinging in her eyes. He had used her, discarded her, ruined her life, and now, after three years of silence, he was cooly suggesting that they have lunch together.

'And what precisely is that supposed to mean?' he asked harshly.

Talia lowered her head, hiding her betraying eyes. She must be careful what she said to him. One careless word in the heat of anger and she might reveal Matty's existence. Alex would pick up on the tiniest clue, that shrewd retentive mind did not miss a thing.

'It doesn't mean anything at all,' she said hurriedly. 'Alex, please, let me go. This is all so pointless, we have nothing to say to each other and——'

'On the contrary, I think we have plenty to say to each other. The choice is yours, Talia—either you lunch with me or I'll give you a lift back to your flat. Either way, we will talk, and I'm sure we won't find your friend Kate so inhospitable.' He sounded bored, immovable, and at the mention of his accompanying her back to the flat, panic almost choked her. She sighed, defeat in every line of her bowed head.

'Surely we can be civilised after three years,' Alex drawled mocking, as the silence lengthened.

'Very well, I'll have lunch with you,' she conceded dully. It was the last thing in the world she wanted to do, but she had been backed into an impossible corner. She had no choice, and her voice revealed that. And yet, all the while, behind her defeat her brain was still working overtime, unable to come up with one single reason as to *why* he should want to spend time with her. It was a complete mystery and rather frightening.

'A fate worse than death?' he teased, quite gently, releasing his biting grip on her arm and propelling her towards the passenger door of his car.

She didn't bother answering that. He had forced her to have lunch with him, but he could not force her to be civil. She slid into the low car in silence, a feeling of impending doom settling in on her as the door closed.

'I have to be back by three,' she told him in a stiff little voice as he slid in beside her, his hard thigh touching hers very briefly before she moved away like a scalded cat, squeezing herself against the door in blind shock.

'As you wish.' His voice gave nothing away, but his powerful hands gripped the wheel too tightly, and the car shot away from the kerb at a frightening speed.

Twenty minutes later they were seated at a secluded table for two in a very expensive, exclusive restaurant, that Talia had only read about before, but had never expected to actually eat at.

'I'm not dressed for this place,' she told him, glancing ruefully at her old, tight jeans. 'Why couldn't we have eaten somewhere smaller, cheaper?'

Alex shrugged uncaringly. 'It's private here. What would you like to drink?'

'Gin and tonic, please,' she said in a small voice, squashed by his coldness. She was not in the least bit hungry, and opening her mouth to tell him so, she abruptly shut it again and ordered a salad. It would probably choke her, but she wouldn't let him see how he was intimidating her.

A deferential waiter took their order, addressing Alex by name, hovering, fussing. He obviously ate

here regularly, she thought, staring down at her
fingernails. At least he hadn't taken her to one of the
restaurants they had frequented when they. . . . Her
thoughts halted. When they what? When she *thought*
they had been so passionately involved? A bitter smile
touched her lips.

Alex was watching her carefully, almost reading her
thoughts, his jaw tightening as he caught that cynical
little smile. 'You're thinner.'

She heard his low voice but did not raise her head.
'Yes.' Her answer was not encouraging.

'But still as beautiful. You look fragile now,
vulnerable.'

'Well, I'm neither fragile or vulnerable,' she told
him sharply, wishing he would stop talking like that.

'And your hair is shorter,' he mused, almost to
himself. 'I remember it used to fall past your waist.'

'Alex, please. . . .' Her face was flushed with
embarrassment.

He stared at her, grey eyes probing, then smiled.
'I'm sorry, I'm embarrassing you.'

'Yes, you are.' She was surprised and flustered by
his apology, sipping her gin as though it was water,
praying it would calm her terrible nerves. 'And if we
have to talk, perhaps you would explain why you've
been telephoning, why you've insisted I have lunch
with you.' She watched as he lit a cheroot, the
movements of his hands easy and graceful.

'I suppose I was intrigued by the way you bolted
from the restaurant the night before last,' he said,
slowly exhaling fragrant smoke from the sensual line
of his mouth.

'I didn't bolt,' she lied protestingly.

'Oh, yes, you did, the moment you saw me.'

'Well, I don't have to explain myself or my actions
to you.' She felt very defensive.

'Of course you don't.' His voice was too smooth, his mouth amused.

Talia lit a cigarette, annoyed that her hand was shaking. It *had* been stupid running away like that, she should have known what his reaction would be.

'I don't understand why my leaving the restaurant should intrigue you,' she said coldly, almost wishing that she had not started this line of questioning.

Alex's dark brows rose. 'Don't you? The more a woman runs, the more a man chases. A fundamental fact of life, I believe,' he added with soft irony.

Talia laughed, a little hysterically. 'And what would you know about women running away from you? Most of them fall at your feet.'

'Not you. You're afraid of me, and I'm trying to find out why.'

She stubbed out her cigarette, feeling suddenly sick. He was too damned perceptive. She glanced at him from beneath her lashes. He was staring at her, his narrowed grey eyes unfathomable. She had no idea what he was thinking, which wasn't fair, because he could read her like a book. She had never been able to work out what was going on behind those cool grey eyes, that had been the cause of her terrible insecurity.

'I'm not at all afraid of you,' she stated, almost evenly. 'I think you flatter yourself.'

The food arrived at that moment and ignoring his mocking amusement, she pretended hungry interest in the salad placed in front of her. She didn't want to talk, she wanted to get away from him—and the sooner the better. It was taking all her willpower and her acting abilities not to reveal how much she hated him, but she realised that it was the only way. Presumably, if she showed her true feelings, he would take her dislike as some sort of personal challenge. She had to act coolly, totally uninterested and then, perhaps, he would leave her alone. After all, she reflected cynically, there were plenty of women whose interest was obvious, and she felt almost certain that Joanna Dominic would still be in his life.

Despite these thoughts, she could not help herself glancing covertly at him as she sipped the excellent wine he had ordered to accompany the food. The charismatic force of his hard looks still pulled her, and more than a few other women in the restaurant, if their discreet glances were anything to go by. She could still remember the hungry touch of his mouth on her body, the smoothness of his skin, the fine roughness of the hair that matted his chest. She could remember everything about his lovemaking, and the memory still had the power to make her ache inside. Her emotions were jumbled, chaotic, and she knew her face revealed them to him.

She sighed heavily, pushing the salad around her plate, knowing that she couldn't touch it.

'I'm not very hungry,' she said with a tight smile, as she finally laid down her knife and fork.

Alex was silent, his face serious. Talia sipped her wine quickly, already feeling its effect on her empty, churning stomach. She glanced obviously at her watch. Kate would be wondering what on earth had happened to her. And there was Matty. . . .

'Are you working at present?' Alex asked suddenly, smoothly refilling her glass.

'No . . . no, but I'm starting a new job at the end of the week.' She chose her words carefully, knowing that this was dangerous ground.

'In advertising?' He was staring at her again and she had the feeling that she had his undivided attention. A devastating prospect.

'Looking after children, actually.' She tried to sound cool.

'You enjoy that kind of work?'

'Obviously,' she retorted sarcastically. Her sarcasm had no effect on him whatsoever, as he continued, 'What made you give up your job with Mark Fitzgerald?'

Talia's heart began to pound sickeningly. His face was totally blank, yet she had the dreadful feeling that he was playing games with her, that he knew something. . . .

'I . . . I found something better,' she said shortly.

'Now why do I get the impression that you're not telling me the truth?'

'I don't have to tell you anything.' She looked at her watch again. 'I really ought to be getting back,' she said, raising her eyes to his, defiance setting her small face.

Alex did not answer, but reached across the table and took her hand in his, his long fingers caressing the fragile bones.

Talia's heart leapt into her throat, his touch making her shiver. She tried to pull her hand away, but his hold on her tightened.

'No wedding ring,' he mused softly. 'Somehow I thought you'd be married by now.'

'No chance.' Her voice was very, very bitter.

Alex stared at her in convincing surprise. 'Why not? You work with children, surely you must want children of your own?'

Talia froze, her body clenching with pain. He must know about Matty, she thought hysterically, that's why he's baiting me like this.

She searched his face, but could find no trace of triumph or amusement, merely surprise and a certain stillness as he waited for her answer.

'I've told you, I'm not the least interested in getting married—now can we drop the subject, please?' she asked stonily, pulling her hand from his.

'How about boy-friends, lovers?' Alex persisted expressionlessly.

She wanted to laugh. She had been unable to let any man near her since Alex. She had loved him so fiercely that her disillusionment, when it came, had frozen her to the core. She distrusted all men and desired no involvement with them. There was only Matty, and her face softened with love as she thought of him. Alex's grey eyes sharpened on her, though he remained silent.

'There's only one person in my life now, there's no room for anybody else,' she told him quietly, realising as soon as the words were spoken that they would be misunderstood. She didn't care. He could think whatever he liked. She had no intention of seeing him again after today.

He stiffened, his jaw clenching. 'I think it's time we left,' he said harshly.

Talia looked at him. He was angry, his eyes as cold as ice. 'I'm ready,' she said, unable to hide her relief.

The hand he slid beneath her elbow as they walked from the restaurant almost crushed her bones, the grip was so tight. She hardly noticed. She was going home, and all she wanted to do was to be able to shut the door on him once and for all, to end the enforced ordeal of being with him.

He drove at a frightening speed through the busy streets. Talia closed her eyes, not wanting to see. He was ominously silent, and casting a glance at his profile, she found it hard and expressionless.

The low car screeched to a halt outside Kate's flat, fifteen minutes later. Talia tried to open the passenger door but couldn't. She turned in her seat to find Alex watching her, his expression dark and brooding. The car buzzed with tension.

'The door won't open,' she said sharply, her nerves

uivering with apprehension at the silver ice in his
yes, at the weird atmosphere.

'It's locked,' he replied impassively, not taking his
yes from her face.

She pulled futilely at the handle. 'Will you unlock
, please?'

'Who is he, Talia, this lover who makes your eyes
elt with tenderness whenever you think of him?'
here was a rough edge to his voice and he ignored
er request. She stiffened, her eyes widening.

'That's none of your damned business,' she said
hakily.

'Once you were mine,' he murmured softly, his eyes
arkening as they rested on the vulnerable line of her
nouth.

'No! I ... I. ... That was over years ago.' She felt
esperate, hating him for even talking about it.

'I can still remember what it felt like to hold you in
ny arms, and however much time and distance you
ut between us, that memory can't be wiped away.
'ou remember it too, I can see it in your eyes,' he said
vith quiet conviction.

'No!' Talia shrank back in her seat, her breathing
insteady. 'I've wiped it from my memory. I don't
vant to remember it, the very thought of it makes me
eel sick!'

'You're a liar.' He smiled at her, and her heart
urned over. His hand reached out and stroked over
er silky hair. 'Shall I prove it to you?'

'Don't touch me, I hate you!' she hissed with
nassionate intensity, watching his mouth tightening,
eeling his fingers closing around a handful of her
uburn hair, tugging on it, pulling back her head. 'No
.. Alex ... please, don't. ...' Her voice was husky
vith fear as she realised his intention and she gasped
vith pain as she tried to move her head.

'Why shouldn't I?' he murmured, staring into h
eyes, his cool clean breath fanning her cheek. 'Yo
already hate me, I have nothing to lose.' He lowere
his dark head slowly, his mouth brushing hers.

Her lips parted to spit out some acid protest and h
possessed them hungrily. As she realised her mistak
her hands pushed at his hard unyielding chest, tea
suddenly rolling down her cheeks.

She could feel the first faint stirrings of respons
aching inside her and she was fighting them, hatin
herself even more than she hated him.

His mouth was gentler now, warm, seeking, hungry
bringing back those deep memories of his swee
expert lovemaking. It was more than she could bear,
tore her apart, and taking him by surprise, she tor
herself from his arms, gasping as her hair was nearl
pulled from its roots.

'Let me out!' she choked, her fingers angrily flickin
away the tears on her face.

'Talia, for God's sake, listen to me——'

'Let me out of this car!' she repeated in a hig
tremulous voice, not looking at him.

She heard him sigh, then his shoulders lifte
sardonically. 'Okay, don't panic.' He pressed a butto
on the dashboard and she found that she could ope
the door. Without a backward glance, she clambere
from the car and ran inside.

CHAPTER THREE

Two days later Talia moved into Leon Miller's house.
It was a hectic rush, and Kate's help was invaluable.
Jake came to pick her up as arranged. Talia was
rushing around collecting the last of Matty's things
when he rang the bell.

Kate answered the door and Talia smiled as they both
entered the room. 'Hello, Jake, it's nice to see you again.'

'Hi, how are you?' he smiled at her, his blue eyes
very bright.

'Flustered,' she answered in reply. Matty was
watching the new arrival with interest, and within
minutes was sitting on Jake's shoulders, chuckling
with delight at having found a new friend.

'Would you like a coffee, Jake?' Kate asked with a
wry smile. 'Talia's bound to be ages.'

They drank coffee and ate biscuits that Kate had
made that morning, then before Talia knew what was
happening, with only time to thank Kate again for all
she had done, and promising to ring, all her
possessions were in the back of the enormous black
car, and she was sitting on the back seat with Matty,
on her way to the house.

Matty was well behaved, wide-eyed at the size of the
car, and Talia, stifling a yawn, gazed out of the
window as they left the city behind. She felt utterly
worn out. She had not slept well the past few nights,
in fact, she hadn't slept well since seeing Alex in that
restaurant. Her thoughts were still unbearably
confused. She could not get the memory of his kiss out
of her mind, it haunted her every moment of the day.

She had been expecting him to ring again, but h
hadn't. She hadn't seen or heard from him sinc
they'd had lunch together. She was glad, she to.
herself. She hated him. She never wanted to see hi
again.

But somehow her vehemence did not ring tru
not even to herself. She felt as though she had bee
asleep for the past three years. Seeing Alex aga
had woken her, made her aware of all the pain an
bitterness still burning inside her. Lunching wit
him had brought the memories crowding bac
memories that she found herself constantly forcin
from her mind.

For the past three years she had been building up
picture of Alex in her mind—he was unfeeling, har
and cruel, selfish, incapable of fidelity and concerne
solely with his own pleasure. She hated him for a
those things. He had used her, tired of her and move
on, not giving a damn that her heart was broken, he
belief in her own judgment shattered. He had left he
miserable and unsure of herself, pregnant and alon
That had been the picture she had been carrying fo
three years, and whenever she had thought of Alex sh
had felt only bitterness and hatred.

Now, since she had met him again, the facts had no
changed, but she had been forced to recognise tha
other side of him, the side she had fallen in love with
He had not been an easy man to get to know, thei
relationship—if that was what one could call it—ha
been brief and sweetly passionate, and Alex had no
talked easily about himself; he was a very private, self
sufficient man. Still, she had learned about him from
things he said, from the way he treated people, from
the way people treated him. She was forced t
remember his kindness, his charismatic charm, hi
gentleness, that he was strong and brilliantly intelligen

nd that he cared about people.

It confused her that her heart twisted whenever she remembered him smiling, making love to her, making her laugh, when she remembered watching him sleep, watching him shower, watching him undress. It was all wrong. She did not love him, she did not even care for him any more, so all those stupid memories should have no effect on her. She should have forgotten. That had almost been true for the past three years, but seeing him again had forced her to realise what a lie she had been living. She had made him a monster in her mind, and now she had to accept that he was a man, a devastatingly attractive man who still had power over her emotions. That was quite a shock. In fact, it made her feel hopelessly depressed, especially when she thought of the future. There was not much to look forward to.

'The kids are dying to meet you.' Jake's enthusiastic voice cut into her bleak reverie, and she turned from the window.

'I'm dying to meet them too,' she smiled, hugging Matty closer. He wriggled away from her, still awe-stricken by the car, his grey eyes wide as he peered out of the window. 'I hope they'll like me.'

'They will,' Jake assured her, his blue eyes briefly meeting hers in the mirror. In no time at all, the car was turning up the long drive, and strangely, Talia felt her nervousness leaving her. She was looking forward to starting this new job; with luck it would be a new life for her.

Leon Miller was at the front door as the car drew up with Belle and Vinnie at his side.

'I'll bring all your stuff, you go and meet the kids,' Jake said cheerfully. Talia slid out of the car, lifting Matty into her arms, and Leon Miller smiled at her, his eyes warm and welcoming.

'It's good to see you,' he drawled, coming toward her.

'I'm very glad to be here,' Talia smiled back at him, meaning every word.

'Let me introduce you to the kids before they pester me to death,' he said drily. 'We haven't had a moment's peace around here since they found out about you.'

So introductions were duly made. Belle was pretty and shy with the same dark blue eyes and dark hair as her father, and Vinnie was strong and precocious and bright, with one tooth missing at the front and untidy blonde hair.

It was fairly obvious that Jake and Belle were children of a previous marriage, while Vinnie had the unmistakable looks of Alicia Miller. In turn, Talia introduced them all to Matty, who was by now drooping tiredly in her arms.

'He looks ready for a nap,' Jake laughed, as Matty dropped the teddy bear he had been clutching so tightly throughout the journey.

'I expect it's all the excitement.' Talia stroked his dark head lovingly.

'Jake will show you to your rooms and when you've put Matty to bed and freshened up, perhaps you would like to join us for coffee,' Leon said as they walked inside.

'Yes, I'd like that.' She could feel the enveloping warmth of the family closing around her, banishing her tiredness and worry.

'Me and Belle will show you your rooms,' Vinnie said loudly, dancing around them as they crossed the hall.

Leon took his hand. 'Talia needs a little time on her own,' he told the little boy. 'You'll see her when she comes down for coffee.'

Vinnie stared at Talia steadily. 'Okay,' he agreed doubtfully, and Talia couldn't help laughing at his solemn sweetness.

Despite protest, Jake insisted on carrying all her belongings upstairs for her. Her rooms were beautiful.

'Do you need any help with Matty?' he asked, dumping her cases on the floor in the bedroom.

'No, I can manage, thank you.'

'I'll see you downstairs later, then.' There was reluctance on his face as he turned to leave.

'Where will you all be?'

'In the lounge.' He opened the door.

'Jake——'. She stopped him before he disappeared. 'Thanks for helping me with my stuff, and thanks for being so kind—today, and at the interview.'

He lifted his young shoulders, his face serious, eyes dark. 'I wanted it to be you, right from the start. I'm glad you've come here.' He was gone before she had time to say anything, and a smile touched her lips as she sat Matty down and gave him a drink.

It was going to work out, she could feel it, and she felt more hopeful than she had done for ages.

While Matty finished his blackcurrant juice, she explored the rooms thoroughly. They were large and spacious, luxuriously furnished. A lounge with a dark carpet and pale walls, the furniture pale leather and dark wood, two bedrooms, one for her with a television, a private telephone and long sunny windows, and a smaller, connecting room for Matty, brightly painted in yellow, the windows thoughtfully barred with wooden animals.

The bathroom was enormous, the suite royal blue porcelain, the walls tiled in blue and white. She couldn't have imagined anything better, and she walked through the rooms smiling with delight at her good fortune.

Matty was asleep before she tucked him in. She kissed his soft, fragrant hair and left the room to shower and change into a pale pink cotton dress, brushing out her shining hair before twisting it into a neat chignon, remembering that Leon Miller had originally wanted an older woman for the job. The chignon made her look older and decidedly more sophisticated, she thought with satisfaction, as she applied mascara to her lashes.

A final glance in the mirror, and a final check on Matty, then she made her way downstairs.

The sound of laughter drew her towards the lounge. The door was open, yet she felt nervous as she hovered near the entrance, not quite sure if she should walk straight in. Turning his head, Jake spotted her. 'Come on in.' He stood up and came towards her, smiling.

Talia walked into the lounge and sat down. Belle and Vinnie were seated on a long couch near the open windows, eating cakes, and Leon Miller was chatting to a younger man sitting by his side.

'Coffee?' Jake stared down at her, his blue eyes serious, telling her that she was beautiful.

'Yes, please.' She refused the sandwiches and cakes he offered, but gratefully sipped the hot coffee.

'Talia, I'd like you to meet Rick Sanbourne.' Leon introduced the young man at his side. 'Rick, this is Talia Montague. She'll be looking after the kids.' He pulled a smiling face at Belle and Vinnie. 'A mammoth task!'

Rick Sanbourne's eyes were appreciative. 'Hi, Talia, pleased to meet you. Leon neglected to tell you that we're cousins and we work together.'

Talia smiled a little warily. 'How do you do, Mr Sanbourne.'

'Rick, please.' He raised his eyebrows at her and she laughed.

'Okay, Rick it is.'

He was tall and slim and dark, in his late twenties, she would have estimated, and now she had been told, she could see a slight family resemblance between the two men. He laughed easily and his brown eyes were charming. She could see that he was ambitious, sure of himself, an elegant young executive. She didn't trust him, but she liked him, she decided as she accepted more coffee from Jake.

Time passed pleasantly in the sunny room and three quarters of an hour had flown by before she realised it, so she excused herself to go and check on Matty, not wanting him to wake alone in a strange place.

She trailed her hands on the polished banisters as she ran upstairs, singing under her breath. She needn't have worried, because Matty was still sleeping peacefully, dead to the world.

She unpacked her own clothes and hung them in the wardrobes, then folded away Matty's into tall chests of drawers in his bright room, and after scattering her few personal possessions around her new lounge, she relaxed in one of the comfortable leather chairs, stretching her long slim legs out in front of her.

It was hot and sunny in the light room and she could feel her eyelids drooping, her mind wandering, lack of sleep catching up with her at last. . . .

The light knocking on the door did not waken her, only the touch of Leon Miller's hand on her shoulder that startled her back to consciousness.

'Alex?' she murmured, still dreaming.

'No, Leon,' came the dry, quiet answer.

Her eyes snapped open then, embarrassed colour washing over her face. 'Oh! I'm sorry. . . .'

'Don't be. I'm intruding.' A slight smile touched the firm line of his mouth.

'No . . . no, really, I shouldn't have fallen asleep.'

She felt very embarrassed. Had she been dreaming of Alex? She couldn't remember. She had spoken his name, and that was bad enough.

'Why not?' His eyes were amused. 'It's pretty tiring work, moving house.'

Talia sat up straight. From where she was sitting she could see Matty still sleeping soundly in his cot.

'What time is it?'

Leon glanced at his watch. 'Six twenty-five.'

Talia sighed. She had been asleep for over an hour. 'I'm sorry. . . .' she began again, feeling that she was not exactly making a good impression on her first day.

'Forget it,' Leon said gently. 'Do you mind if I sit down?'

'Please——' She indicated one of the chairs next to hers. 'I didn't mean to be so rude ... I. . . .' She halted, flustered.

Leon watched her. 'Are you nervous?'

'Very,' she admitted honestly. 'I did so want to make a good impression on my first day.'

'As far as I'm concerned you have. Your actual work doesn't start until tomorrow anyway, so today your time is your own. I only came up to make sure you have everything you need, and that you find your rooms suitable.' He lit a cigarette before continuing, 'And to explain that I intended picking you up myself today, but unfortunately I was held up by an important phone call.' He laughed. 'Jake volunteered.'

Talia smiled, relaxing again, liking him. 'The rooms are lovely—I didn't expect so much space to myself. You have a beautiful home.'

'Not beautiful enough, it would seem.' The sudden harsh note in his voice brought her head up.

'I don't understand. . . .'

'That was another reason I wanted to talk to you. I don't doubt that you've heard the rumours about my marriage, the newspapers have been full of them, and if you're going to be looking after the children you ought to know the truth.'

'Oh, no, really, you don't have to explain anything to me.' His face gave nothing away, yet she knew that he felt pain and her heart went out to him.

'I just want you to know that it was my fault as much as Alicia's. The newspapers don't give that impression at all, and I wanted to set the record straight, right from the start.' His voice was dry.

Talia twisted her hands together in her lap. He was still in love with his wife, that was very obvious, and she knew all about love turned sour.

'I think I understand how you must feel,' she said gently.

'Yes, I really think you do.' He got to his feet, pushing a hand through his dark hair. 'To get on to less maudlin topics of conversation, dinner is at eight—we usually dress, but nothing too formal. Oh, and by the way, welcome.'

'Thank you.' Her smile was bright and beautiful.

He turned and left the room and she felt warm and happy. As she looked through her wardrobe for something suitable to wear for dinner she couldn't help wondering about Alicia and Leon. It was so sad and painful when a marriage split up.

She liked Leon Miller a great deal, even though she had known him such a short time. She had seen behind that hard, businesslike exterior, had seen the family man beneath. He was warm, generous, and there seemed to be that strange understanding between them that sometimes, though rarely, occurs when people meet. She felt she could go to him with any problem she had. Any problem except Alex.

She sat down on the soft bed, her clothes suddenly forgotten. What on earth was the matter with her?

Alex was not a problem at all. It was doubtful she would even see him again. It was all wishful thinking.

Perhaps that was what had formed the immediate bond between Leon Miller and herself. Both had lost the person they loved, both recognised it in each other. She felt a rush of tears filling her eyes. Why couldn't she put Alex out of her mind? Why did she remember every moment, every detail of the time they spent together?

Even now she could remember what he had been wearing that very first evening he took her out. She remembered the doorbell ringing at precisely eight o'clock, and her stomach clamouring with nerves. Alex had been outside, taking her breath away as she opened the door. His suit had been dark and formal, expensively tailored to his wide shoulders, the waistcoat taut over the muscled flatness of his stomach. His grey eyes had been warm, narrowed, caressing as he greeted her, and Talia had responded deeply, drawn to him without even thinking.

That evening passed in a haze, she had no idea what she ate or drank in that expensive restaurant. Alex had made her laugh, eased her slight fear of him, and his innate charm had knocked her sideways.

She had talked unselfconsciously about herself and had learned about him. He was totally different from how she had imagined him. The press hung round him like flies, the newspapers reporting his every move, his every affair. He was tough and successful, wealthy and attractive, and his women were equally beautiful, intelligent and successful.

But during that first evening Talia spent with him, she even forgot to wonder why he was spending his time with an eighteen-year-old nobody like herself. He drove her back to her flat. It was very late, the streets almost deserted. He kissed her mouth briefly, his lips hard and sensual, then left.

Talia was surprised and a little disappointed, but her mind had been filled with him from that moment on, her heart lost so easily. She was flattered by his attention, already in love, and he was so unlike anybody she had ever met before.

During the weeks that followed, he pursued her openly, sweeping her off her feet. He took her to films, to the theatre, to parties and exhibitions, on boat trips and long drives in the countryside, and during those wonderful times, he never did more than kiss her. Her life was a breathless, happy dream, and she was totally innocent until that last beautiful night.

She had been over it a million times in her mind. She was at home, exhausted after a particularly hectic day at work, just stepping out of the bath, when the doorbell rang.

Pulling on a thin silk robe, she ran to answer it, her wet auburn hair cascading loosely down her back. It was Alex. She was surprised yet so happy to see him, and her eyes lit up as she opened the front door.

'Can I come in?' he asked, with a slow easy smile.

'Yes . . . yes, of course.' She felt the colour pouring into her face as his cool grey eyes slid over her wet body and the clinging silk of her robe.

'I wasn't expecting you . . .' she began falteringly. 'I. . . .'

'Talia, shut up and let me in,' he said with gentle mockery.

She opened the door wide, her heart tripping over itself as he stepped inside.

He walked straight into the lounge and she followed, watching him hungrily. He was wearing tight jeans, the faded denim clinging to his lean hips, and a thin blue shirt.

'I'll just get dressed,' she murmured, her mouth dry. 'Help yourself to a drink.'

She turned to leave the room, but he caught her hand, staring down at her with unreadable eyes.

'I like you the way you are.' His voice was low, very deep and her heart almost stopped beating.

'Won't you sit down?' she whispered, her voice deserting her.

Alex smiled and said softly, 'I wanted to see you. I have to go away tomorrow.'

'Away?' Her eyes widened in dismay and in an effort to hide her feelings she walked over to the sideboard and poured out two measures of whisky, adding soda to her own.

Alex's eyes were serious as she handed him a glass. 'I have to fly to South America,' he explained, watching her carefully. 'A close friend of mine has been shot dead. He runs one of my companies over there, so I have to go.'

'Yes, yes, of course.' Talia bit her lip, horrified by what he told her. 'Why was he shot?'

Alex shrugged gracefully. 'There's a lot of fighting going on there at the moment, rebel forces against the government—it's crazy!' He raked a hand through the darkness of his hair and Talia noticed how tired he looked. There were lines of strain around his beautifully moulded mouth, his powerful body tense.

'I'm so sorry about your friend,' she said softly, her eyes dark with love for him.

Alex stared at her. 'So am I,' he muttered, throwing back the contents of the glass he held in one mouthful, the muscles of his throat contracting. 'He was a good man, a good friend.'

'Won't you sit down? You look so tired,' she suggested gently, wishing that there was something she could say or do to make him feel better.

Alex smiled slightly and coiled indolently into one of the comfortable chairs. Talia sank on to the couch, pulling the silk robe more tightly around her damp body. She felt utterly miserable.

'How . . . how long will you be away?' As soon as she asked, she immediately wished she hadn't. She didn't want to sound possessive, even though she felt she would die without him.

'I can't tell,' he replied expressionlessly. 'I have to sort out the funeral arrangements, sort out the company business—it could take a week, it could take months.' He lit two cigarettes and handed one to her.

Talia watched him smoke, and suddenly realised that she was crying, silent tears pouring down her face, blurring her vision.

She turned away as Alex saw them, heard him swearing softly, then his hands closed on her shoulders and he pulled her to her feet and into his arms. 'Oh God, don't cry, Talia.'

'I'm sorry,' she sniffed against his chest. 'It's just that I'll miss you so. . . .'

He sighed heavily. 'I'll miss you too—I'd take you with me if it wasn't so damned dangerous.'

'I wouldn't mind——' she began, her heart suddenly bursting with happiness because he would miss her, because he wanted her with him.

'But I would,' he muttered against her wet hair. 'There's no way I could put you in that kind of danger.' He tilted up her face and kissed her wet eyes, his tongue licking away the salty tears. 'Talia——'

Their eyes met as he murmured her name, glances locking fiercely, and awareness like pure electricity shot through Talia's body.

They stared at each other for endless moments, then, suddenly, Alex's mouth parted hers with a hunger that melted her against the taut strength of his body, his arms tightening around her.

He kissed her deeply, expertly, his mouth hungry

and sensual, then trailed gentle kisses across her cheeks, her chin, her eyelids.

'I've tried to keep away from you, Talia,' he murmured roughly against her lips. 'But I can't, I want you—so badly.'

She smiled, her dark eyes radiant. She had been afraid he did not find her attractive, and now she knew that his restraint had been for her sake. Love for him was aching inside her as she slid her slim arms up around his neck. After tonight, she would not see him for God knows how long, she could not bear him to leave her.

'I want you too,' she whispered against his brown throat.

The eyes that met hers were shadowed, burning with desire, questioning—until he saw her answer. Then he lifted her into his arms, effortlessly carrying her to her bed, kicking shut the bedroom door.

He laid her gently on the bed, and arched over her, his long strong fingers parting the silken robe, his breath coming raggedly as he stared at her slender white body.

He saw the colour flushing her face as he devoured her nakedness, and smiled tenderly. 'You're beautiful,' he said huskily, gently touching the satiny skin of her stomach. 'Your skin is so white, so soft, I'm almost afraid to touch you.'

'Alex, hold me,' she begged, closing her eyes.

With a groan he brought his hard body down beside her, his mouth finding hers again, his hands beginning their sensual exploration of her body.

She unbuttoned his shirt, pulling it from his wide tanned shoulders, her breath catching sharply as she stared at the taut, powerful lines of his hair-roughened chest, at the heavy muscles of his arms.

Since the first moment of their meeting, everything

had been building up to this. She felt weak and hot, aching sensations flooding her body. Alex's mouth was at her throat, warm, hungry, his hands moving slowly to cup her breasts, the nipples stiffening beneath the delicate brush of his fingertips.

She arched her body to his hands and lips, her own hands clenching against the smooth skin of his shoulders, her blood molten in her veins, roaring in her ears, needing him so desperately now.

He aroused her patiently, with hungry expertise, his mouth against her heated skin, touching every inch of her body, until she was writhing beneath him, moaning softly, lost to everything but her desire for him.

When he took her trembling body into his arms again, she realised that he was naked, the hard smoothness of his skin somehow cool and deeply satisfying against her own burning flesh.

He took both her hands in his, placing them against his chest. 'Touch me,' he ordered raggedly. 'Touch me as I touched you.'

Desperate to obey, she felt him shaking as she explored his body, running her fingers through the mat of fine hair on his chest, her lips following the path of her hands.

His skin tasted faintly salty, the clean erotic male scent going to her head like strong wine. His body was magnificent, smooth tanned skin, taut heavy muscles, his stomach flat and hard, his legs powerful, rough with hair.

She felt him shuddering beneath her caresses, his heart racing, his skin damp with sweat, and she lost herself in the hard beauty of him, delighting in the power she had to make him groan and catch his breath.

He pulled her back into the circle of his arms again

when the sweet innocence of her lovemaking became almost too much to bear, his mouth touching hers again, his hands stroking over her until she was pleading for his possession.

Then he moved over her, his clenched body parting her silken thighs, still kissing her, still caressing her to ease that first painful moment of possession, and when the climax came, Talia clung to him, her nails raking his skin, lost in the all-consuming pleasure that blanked out her mind and tore her body apart.

Afterwards she lay against his chest, his arms possessively tight around her, her body still aching with pleasure, her heart filled with love for him.

They stared at each other. Alex's grey eyes were dark, glazed, very gentle. They talked for a while, their voices drugged, quiet, then Talia suddenly drifted into sleep, languorously happy.

Alex lazily smoked a cigarette, watching her as she lay in his arms, then he too gave himself up to the darkness of sleep.

In the cool light of dawn he woke her with a slow sweet hunger that exploded into an ecstasy that left them clinging to each other.

And in the morning he left early, kissing her fiercely, almost desperately, promising to ring her.

Talia smiled and made coffee for him, trying to pretend that she wasn't utterly miserable and depressed.

As soon as he had gone, she burst into tears, some sixth sense warning her of disaster. She tried to tell herself that he wouldn't be gone for ever, but when she remembered the piercing sweetness of the previous night spent in his arms, she felt sure that nothing so fiercely beautiful could last for very long.

She had still been crying when the telephone rang. It had been Alex from the airport.

'Hell, Talia, I miss you already,' he had growled roughly, his voice sounding so far away.

I love you, she had whispered silently, wishing she had the courage to tell him out loud.

And when she thought about the sheer hell of that morning and all the mornings since then, she reminded herself that at least she had never admitted her love to him. She had been saved that final humiliation. In her heart, though, she knew it was a hollow victory.

CHAPTER FOUR

THE following month flew past, and Talia found working for Leon Miller very enjoyable. She was getting to know the family well, getting on marvellously with the children. Matty loved it too. Belle seemed to have a special affection for him, which over the weeks became mutual. They were never apart, and all Matty's conversations began to include, 'Belle says——' and 'Belle showed me——'

Talia's friendship with Leon was deepening too. When he was at home they often spent the late evening talking together, usually with Jake, if he wasn't out with his friends. Talia felt safe with Leon. He was still in love with his wife, which left him totally uninterested in sexual diversion. He was the first man, since Alex, she had let into her confidence. Any man approaching her, or showing any interest, she froze off. She could not trust them after Alex's betrayal, and her deep feelings for him, whether they were love or hatred, left no room for any other involvement.

Yes, everything was better than she had dared to hope for, she thought, as she sat by the swimming pool, relaxing in the sun.

It had been a wonderfully hot summer and spending so much of the past month in the garden had left her skin with a faint golden tan.

From where she was sitting, she could see Matty playing with Belle. Vinnie was away for the week. He had pestered Leon into sending him to a special summer camp in Scotland. The house was empty, because Leon himself was away on business in France. He was expected back that afternoon. Talia felt calm and happy.

'Hi, I've brought you some coffee.' Rick's voice beside her turned her head and she watched with a smile as he sat down opposite her.

'Thank you.' She took the tray from him and poured coffee for them both. 'Just got back?'

Rick had been away in New York for the past four days. He worked for Leon and lived at the house whenever he was in England.

'Yes, and I'm exhausted. How have things been here?'

'Fine—this house runs like clockwork. That's why I've got plenty of time to laze around the pool,' she told him with a smile.

She liked him, but she was still a little wary of him. He did not hide the fact that he found her attractive, and that predatory gleam she sometimes caught in his brown eyes worried her, but she knew she could handle him. She had met Rick's type before. He chased women automatically, but it was all lighthearted, a game to him. He had asked Talia out a number of times, but she had turned him down. He didn't care and he hadn't given up.

'You've settled in okay, then?' He offered her a cigarette, which she took.

'Yes, I love it here.' Her sincerity was obvious.

Rick leaned back in his seat, his eyes resting lazily on Belle and Matty, who were both lying in the long grass. 'The kids love you, they seem much happier since you came.'

Talia smiled at the compliment. 'They weren't unhappy before, though, surely?'

'It was one hell of a difficult time when Alicia walked out. Leon was out of his mind, and the kids were scared to death. There was also quite a lot of trouble with the press—pestering the kids when they went to school, hounding Leon every time he left the house—that sort of thing.' He drew deeply on his cigarette, not looking at her.

Talia shook his head. 'How awful for them! I hadn't realised how bad it was.'

'It can't be easy if your mother walks out on you in a blaze of publicity. Vinnie was inconsolable, and Belle took it very badly—she looks on Alicia as her mother.'

'I don't know how she could have done it,' said Talia, half to herself, knowing that she could never leave Matty, whatever the circumstances.

'Her reasons were good enough.' Rick's voice was suddenly rather sharp, and Talia flushed.

'I'm sorry,' she said uneasily, sensing his lightning change of mood. 'I didn't mean to criticise. . . .'

'Of course you didn't. I shouldn't have jumped down your throat.' His eyes veered away from hers, his expression uncomfortable, and Talia realised something in that second.

'You loved her,' she said gently, very surprised.

Rick lit another cigarette. 'What a clever girl you are.' His voice was flat but not unkind. 'Yes, I love her. I've loved her ever since I first met her with Leon, and she—she hardly knows I exist.' He laughed without humour.

Talia frowned and touched his arm, gently. 'I'm sorry,' she apologised again. 'I shouldn't have been prying.'

Rick's hand closed over hers and she did not draw away. 'It's good to tell somebody about it. Alicia knows, of course, she used me shamelessly whenever they rowed. I should have got out of here as soon as it started, I suppose, but even then it was too late.'

Talia didn't know what to say. She stared at him in

silence, feeling rather shocked. Alicia Miller held so many hearts, so uncaringly. Rick was young and handsome, he was making a name for himself in business. When she had first met him, she would never have guessed that he was tearing himself apart with love for his cousin's wife. That fast, predatory routine was merely a shield for his pride. It was all so depressing.

At that moment she could not think of one single person who was happy in their love affairs. Perhaps that was just how it happened, she thought miserably. Kate, Leon, Rick, herself—perhaps everybody who fell in love was doomed to failure and pain.

She wanted to say something cheering to Rick, something that would maybe stop him hurting so much—but there was nothing she could say. She suddenly felt sorry that she had treated him so warily, so suspiciously.

'I've made you miserable,' he apologised, his smile not quite reaching his eyes. He squeezed her hand. 'I don't know what it is about you, Talia, you have a talent for eliciting secrets.'

Talia smiled, liking him, sensing that he was rather embarrassed by what he had revealed.

'You needn't worry, I won't tell a soul,' she promised truthfully.

'Won't tell a soul what?' Jake had appeared beside them, sliding his lean body into one of the cane chairs, his eyes narrowing on their clasped hands, then moving to Talia's face, serious, questioning.

'Mind your own business,' she told him, softening the words with a smile. 'Do you want some coffee?'

'I guess so.'

'How's tricks, Jake?' Rick asked easily.

'Fine.' There was a sullen edge to his young voice, as though he was going to push the issue of Talia and

Rick further. But at that moment, Belle spotted him, calling him over to show him something she and Matty had found.

Talia watched him stroll over to the children.

'Very protective, isn't he?' Rick remarked with amusement. 'I reckon you've made a definite conquest there.'

Talia pulled a wry face. 'I hope not, I wouldn't want to hurt him.'

Rick touched her cheek. 'You're too young to be so serious,' he said lightly, and got to his feet. 'I'd better get on with some work before Leon gets back. See you later.'

He walked back towards the house, leaving Talia deep in thought.

Leon returned late in the afternoon. Talia was out with the children. Between them, she and Jake had managed a fairly controlled afternoon trip to the zoo. Matty had spent practically the whole afternoon on Jake's shoulders, Belle and Talia had walked hand in hand, laughing together.

By the time they got back it was almost seven, and Matty was already asleep. On seeing the long black car, Jake and Belle disappeared to find Leon as soon as they got in, and Talia fed Matty and put him to bed, then showered and changed for dinner, choosing a beautifully-cut dress in thin, printed autumn-coloured silk. She was just brushing out her hair when somebody knocked on her door. It was Leon.

'Hello.' She smiled at him warmly.

'Are you busy?' He had changed for dinner, the dark velvet of his jacket vivid against his white shirt, his hair still damp from the shower.

He was very attractive, she thought, her eyes assessing as she looked at him, but he had no effect on her heart at all.

Four years ago, a man as attractive as he was would have aroused her interest; now she hardly acknowledged men's existence at all, except with wary, careful suspicion.

When she looked at Leon, she could see his attraction, but her warmth was for the friendship they shared. She supposed it was quite strange that such a close friendship had flourished so quickly between a man in his early forties and a girl in her early twenties. But it had happened, they had recognised something in each other that had drawn them together. Kindred spirits, perhaps.

'No, not at all,' she replied, laying down her brush. 'Come in.'

Leon sat down. 'I'm exhausted,' he said with a rueful smile. 'I seem to have been travelling all week.'

'Successful trip?' Talia slid a gold bangle on to her wrist.

'Very successful.' He pulled a small package out of his pocket. 'And this is for you.'

She took it from him in surprise, wondering what it could be.

'Oh, you shouldn't——'

'Before you say it,' he cut in, 'I bought each of the children a present and I couldn't leave you out. There's also a little something for Matty downstairs.'

Talia pulled open the package and found a small bottle of French perfume. She lifted the stopper and sniffed the fragrance. It was light and sophisticated.

'It's lovely—thank you. I'll wear it tonight,' she smiled, dabbing it on to her pulse spots, touched by his kindness.

'Has everything been running smoothly? Any problems?' He reached for his cigarette case, offering her one which she refused, lighting one for himself. Talia thought for a moment, then shook her head.

'No. Vinnie got off to Scotland okay, after a last-minute panic. Belle and Matty are still getting on wonderfully. Oh, yes, and we all went to the zoo this afternoon.'

'I heard,' Leon smiled.

'Well, that's about it. Everything has been fine. I was telling Rick—this house runs like a well-oiled clock.'

'You didn't mind being left alone to cope with everything?' he asked, genuinely concerned.

'No, I enjoyed the peace, I suppose. I might as well admit that I haven't been working very hard while you've been away, I've spent most of the time lazing in the garden sunbathing. And of course, I had Jake and Mrs Rodale to help me.'

Leon smiled. 'Jake is very fond of you, very protective.'

'That's what Rick said.' Talia suddenly felt worried. 'You don't think . . .?'

'You're young and you're beautiful, he's bound to be a little in love with you,' Leon told her in a soft amused, totally unworried drawl.

'I hope not.' Talia didn't believe him, and she brushed aside his compliments. In her experience love was the one thing she did *not* inspire in men. Alex had taught her that lesson very well.

'Why?' He regarded her through a haze of smoke. 'It's all part of growing up. He'll get over his infatuation—don't worry about it.' He laughed. 'Listen to me—I sound like an old man! It's so easy to forget that there's only a few years between you and Jake.'

Talia grimaced. 'Awful, isn't it? I feel years older.'

Leon's eyes were suddenly gentle. 'I guess having a child so young must have rocketed you into instant maturity.'

She nodded in frowning silence. Rick's remarks that afternoon came back into her mind. Twenty-two. When she said it to herself, it sounded young, yet she did not feel twenty-two. She was much older and more experienced than most girls of that age. It worried her, made her think she was somehow missing out on life and youth.

Leon stood up, moved towards her and took both her hands in his. 'Now I've upset you.'

She shook her head, smiling suddenly. 'No, of course you haven't. I've just realised how lucky I am to have a friend like you.'

It was the truth, he *had* became a very special friend. Age didn't matter at all.

Leon was touched, pleased by her words; she could see it in his dark blue eyes as he bent his head, his mouth touching her cheek. Neither heard the door swinging open behind them, nor the tall beautiful blonde woman entering the room, stopping in surprise at what she saw in front of her.

'How very touching!' Her words were sweet but hard, and Talia nearly jumped out of her skin.

Leon turned slowly, his face giving nothing away as he stared at his wife.

'Alicia, what the hell are you doing here?' he demanded in a low voice.

'Interrupting something, by the look of it.' Alicia Miller smiled, her beauty taking Talia's breath away. 'Really, Leon, what a greeting!'

'And what did you expect?' He was totally impassive, and if Talia had not known better, she would have been convinced that he did not give a damn about his wife.

'I certainly didn't expect to find you in somebody else's arms so soon.' Her voice was too light, too brittle. 'Aren't you going to introduce us, darling?'

Leon's jaw tensed and Talia realised that he was very angry.

I shouldn't be here, she thought desperately. This has nothing to do with me, I'm intruding on something very private. So before Leon had time to speak she stepped forward, smiling tentatively.

'Mrs Miller, I'm Talia Montague. Leon has employed me to look after the children. I'm sure you want to be alone, so if you'll excuse me. . . .' She cursed her voice for sounding so stilted, so embarrassed, and moved quickly from the room, breathing a sigh of relief when she shut the door, thankful that neither had said anything more, or tried to detain her.

She wandered downstairs and out into the garden, lost in thought about what had just happened. Was Alicia Miller back for good? If so, where did that leave her?

She shook her head. There was no point worrying, until she knew for sure. At least the children would be happy.

She wandered round the garden, trying to work things out, so engrossed that she turned a corner and cannoned straight into Jake, because she wasn't looking where she was going.

He reached out and steadied her, his hands closing on her shoulders, fingers almost caressing.

She looked up into his face, her eyes blank for a second. 'I'm sorry, I wasn't looking.' Her slight smile was apologetic.

He released her, his eyes dark, serious. 'Why so worried?'

He fell in step beside her and Talia glanced at him, absently thinking how attractive he was, tall and lean and very much like Leon.

'Don't you know that Mrs Miller is here?'

'Alicia? You're kidding!' His surprise was obvious.

'No. I think she's just arrived.'

'Does Leon know?' There was something in his voice, something she could not read. Anger? Disappointment?

She nodded. 'I was talking to him when she came in.'

Jake was silent for a moment, then he asked, 'Is she back for good?'

'Jake, I don't know anything—I came out here. It's none of my business.' She heard him swearing under his breath and asked, 'What's the matter?'

'He'll take her back, I know he will.' His young face was set, frowning.

'Don't you get on with her?' It was a tentative question. She was puzzled by his reaction.

'She's okay, I suppose.' He stopped walking, leaning back against a tree trunk, his fingers scraping over the rough bark. 'But you didn't see him when she walked out. It was almost as bad as when my mother died—nobody could get through to him, and I don't want to see him like that again—it's so unfair!'

Talia wasn't sure what to say to him. He was angry and hurt, and there was nothing she could do to help.

'Leon cares for her. I think he wants her back,' she said quietly, telling him the truth.

Jake stared at her. 'I know,' he admitted heavily. 'And I want him to be happy. It's just that—oh, I don't know.' He turned away from her, gazing across the garden. 'My mother died when I was nine—a car accident. Leon was out of his mind with grief—he was a different man. I was too young to really understand. When he met Alicia, he sort of—got back to normal, if you see what I mean. I was glad when they got married. She was always kind to us, especially to Belle because she was so small. When she had Vinnie, she had to give up her job for a while. She hated that, and that was when the rows started. She went back to modelling, of course, but with Leon being away so much. . . . I don't know what was happening between them, but things got worse and worse, until she walked out a couple of months ago and there was all that newspaper stuff about that singer.' He sighed, his face twisting. 'I could see the same pain in Leon, the same grief as when my mother died. I don't want him to be hurt again—it's so bloody unfair, he doesn't deserve it.'

Talia stared at the long lean sweep of his back, her heart aching for him. He was hurting so much for his father.

'Perhaps she'll stay this time,' she said quietly.

Jake shrugged. 'And if she doesn't?' He did not turn round.

'There's nothing you can do, Jake. Leon knows what he wants, you can only be there if he needs you.' She knew it was inadequate, but what else could she say? It was always so obvious to someone on the outside of a relationship. They could look in so easily and see what was wrong, see people making disastrous decisions, crazy decisions that could wreck their lives. It was like watching a film where one of the characters was standing in the middle of the road, a car hurtling towards them. You knew they were going to be hit, but you couldn't warn them.

Jake's protective attitude to his father was very touching, very sweet, but Talia knew that Leon loved his wife. He would be unable to use his pride to send her away. She sighed, and moved towards Jake, gently touching his shoulder. 'It must be time for dinner. We ought to go in.'

He turned slowly, and she saw the lonely pain in his eyes and suddenly understood. He had been denied a mother very young and he was still afraid that Alicia would take his father away. Obviously Alicia had never bothered to soothe or allay those fears—no, that was unfair, she told herself, halting her thoughts. But it didn't change the fact that Jake was staring at her with dark eyes that told her just how unsure and alone and young he was.

Almost instinctively her arms went around him. She couldn't bear his suffering. His own arms closed around her tightly, his dark head bent to her shoulder as they stood together in the soft summer dusk of the garden, knowing the nameless comfort of closeness.

She clung to the hard lean strength of his body, closing her eyes, feeling calmer, stronger.

At last Jake raised his head, his serious eyes not quite meeting hers. 'Thanks,' he said huskily, and she could see that he was a little embarrassed as he released her.

'Thank you.' She smiled back at him, dissolving the last of the embarrassment between them. She slid her arm through his and they walked back towards the house.

Dinner that evening was something of a disaster. Jake was morosely silent throughout the meal, and Rick, too, hardly said a word. His eyes were on Alicia, who burned like a brilliant light in a dark room, as she laughed with Belle and flirted unashamedly with Leon.

Talia watched them all, her appetite small, the undercurrents in the dining room almost tangible, getting to her.

Leon tried to include her in the conversations swirling around the table, but she found her usual brightness gone, and a terrible insecurity held her almost silent in its grip, as she wondered about her future. Alicia's eyes were curious, wary, whenever they rested on her. It wasn't a good sign.

She escaped as soon as she could after the meal, on the pretext of checking on Matty. It was a relief to leave the strained atmosphere and retire to the peace of her own rooms, although the solitude did not help her restless mood.

Leon came to see her an hour later.

'You looked so miserable at dinner,' he said with a faint smile.

'No, honestly. . . .' she lied with too much emphasis.

He walked over to the open windows, staring out over the dim gardens. 'Alicia wants to come back here, start again,' he said, getting straight to the point.

Talia digested that without surprise. It was what she had suspected the first moment she had seen Alicia.

'And you?' she asked quietly.

'I want her.' He did not bother to disguise his need.

'I hope it works out for both of you.' There was a catch in her voice as she spoke. She wanted Leon to be happy.

'I'm under no illusions this time.' He turned from the windows and smiled at her. 'I wanted you to know that you won't lose your job if Alicia stays.'

'But you won't need me. . . .' she began, biting her lower lip, her eyes worried.

'Of course we will. I'll be working, Alicia will be working. Your job here is safe, Talia, for as long as you want it.'

'Does Mrs Miller agree?' she asked, still not quite daring to be relieved.

'Yes.' His one word answer was firm and immediate, but for some reason she was sure that he was not quite telling the truth.

'You're very kind,' she said huskily.

Leon shook his head, smiling. 'You do an excellent job here, the kids would be lost without you.' Talia laughed, pleased, almost believing him.

When she finally got to bed, she found that she could not sleep. The old insecure worries that she had thought behind her came crowding in on her in the dark, despite Leon's reassurances.

She was almost sure that Alicia did not like her, did not want her in the house and the innocently compromising position she had found them in on her arrival had not helped. And if Alicia wanted her gone. . . .

She tried to blot the problem from her mind. There was no point in worrying about something that hadn't even happened yet.

As on every other night, as she finally drifted towards sleep, Alex's lean dark face swam into her mind. She dreamt of him nearly every night, sometimes waking with tears on her face. She couldn't understand it. Why did she dream of him? She *didn't* care for him.

She turned on her side, pushing her face into the cool pillow, wishing he would stop haunting her.

On her way down to breakfast the next morning she met Rick on the stairs.

'Hi, you're looking beautiful this morning.' He took her arm and Matty's hand.

The little boy stared up at him, smiling.

'Hello, Rick.' Her eyes were warm. 'You're looking very smart.'

'Ah, that's because I'm off to Munich on the ten o'clock flight. Business calls.' His voice was a little too light and Talia cast him a searching glance. 'Got it in one,' he said wryly, catching that glance and understanding it. 'I'm moving out.'

'It must be awful for you,' Talia said gently, almost knowing how he was feeling.

Rick shrugged, still smiling. 'I should have done it long before now.'

'Good luck,' she said gravely. Of course it was the only thing he could do, loving Alicia as he did, but it was very sad.

'I'll see you again, you silly, serious girl.'

As they walked into the dining room, Jake, Leon and Belle greeted them.

'Good morning, Talia.' Leon's eyes searched her face as she sat down.

'Good morning, everyone.' Her bright smile included them all.

'We're all going to the seaside!' Belle told her excitedly.

'And you're very welcome to come with us,' Leon added.

'Yes, do come,' said Jake, watching her as she poured out some milk for Matty.

'Do you need me?' she asked Leon. It sounded suspiciously like a family outing, some kind of reunion, perhaps.

'We don't need you in your professional capacity,' he told her with a wide smile, 'but we would be very glad to have you along.'

Luckily Matty wasn't listening to the conversation, he was singing to himself, engrossed in his little boy's thoughts. Talia didn't want to have to disappoint him.

'I have a lot to do, so I won't bother, thank you,' she said politely.

'Take the day off, then,' Leon suggested wickedly, and when she opened her mouth to protest, added, 'I insist. There'll be nothing for you to do here.'

'You're spoiling the girl, my darling.' Alicia's low amused voice swung Talia's head round. She had not noticed Leon's wife entering the room.

'On the contrary, we're all trying to persuade her to come with us,' Leon said drily, as Alicia sat down, reaching for the coffee.

She was so beautiful, Talia thought without envy. She had the face of an angel, her blonde hair drifting around her shoulders, her curved body wrapped seductively in cream satin. Somehow she managed to make Talia feel dowdy, childish and rather stupid merely by being in the same room.

'I should leave her alone, darling. She seems perfectly capable of making her own decisions.' Alicia's pale blue eyes slid with bored blankness over Talia and the child by her side.

Jake muttered something under his breath, his chair scraping loudly on the tiled floor as he stood up and left the room.

Talia sipped her coffee in an embarrassed, uncomfortable silence, giving Matty his breakfast at the same time.

Belle was chattering to anyone who would listen. 'Vinnie will be so *mad* when he finds out we've been to the seaside!'

'Then we will have to go again when he gets back from camp,' Leon drawled, watching Talia, while Alicia watched him.

As soon as Matty had finished, she stood up and lifted him into her arms. 'Excuse me——' she said to nobody in particular.

'We'll be going after breakfast,' Leon told her. 'And I meant what I said—take the day off.'

Talia flashed him a quick smile and left the room. Whatever Leon said about the safety of her job, Alicia was making it perfectly clear that she was not happy with the situation.

She met Jake on the landing. He opened the door of her rooms for her, as she had her hands full with Matty.

'You won't change your mind?' he asked darkly.

'No, I'm going to visit Kate,' said Talia, making the decision on the spur of the moment.

'It was Alicia, wasn't it? She didn't want you to come, she put you off.' He was frowning, his lean face angry.

'No, Jake, it wasn't like that at all. It's a day for your family to be together, to re-establish friendships. It's nothing to do with me, I would have been an intruder,' she explained with a smile.

Jake sighed. 'I still wish you'd come, it won't be the same without you. I want to be with you.'

'Well, I'll see you when you get back.' She kept her voice purposely light, and turning round a few seconds later, found herself alone. He had gone in silence.

She spent the afternoon at Kate's flat. Kate was bright and friendly and avid for details about Talia's job. The time flew by pleasantly and she and Matty didn't get back to the house until after six.

Dashing into the kitchen before getting changed, to fetch Matty a glass of milk, she found Mrs Rodale in the midst of almost frantic preparations, up to her elbows in flour.

'Hello, Mrs Rodale, you look busy,' she remarked, opening the refrigerator door.

'Visitors,' Mrs Rodale replied dourly.

'How many?' Talia was sure it must be well over ten.

'Only two.' Mrs Rodale actually smiled. 'But they're important, so Mr Miller says. Business.'

Talia laughed. Jake had told her that Mrs Rodale had been their cook and housekeeper ever since they moved to England. She was round and middle-aged, with a kind heart, a stern face and a dry tongue. All the children adored her.

'What time is dinner?' she asked.

'They're arriving at eight or thereabouts,' she was informed. 'Dinner will be any time after eight-thirty.'

'Are the others back?' Talia watched Matty drinking his milk with loving eyes.

'No sign of them,' Mrs Rodale said grimly, working away as she talked. 'And they'd better hurry!'

Talia gave Matty his tea, bathed him and read him a story before tucking him up in bed. Then she took a quick shower, dried her hair and made up her face, trying to decide what to wear. When friends or business associates were invited for dinner, dress was usually formal, so she chose a special dress, black taffeta with a flaring ruffled skirt and a tight bodice. It complemented her faintly golden skin and gave fire to her burnished hair which she left loose, falling around her bare shoulders. She looked good, she realised without any particular pleasure.

She checked that Matty was sleeping soundly, then made her way downstairs to the lounge where she could hear talking, laughter. She pushed open the doors, totally unprepared for the sight that met her eyes—Alex Jordan, laughing with Alicia, lounging indolently in one of the comfortable chairs.

Her eyes widened, her heart lurched sickeningly. It can't be! she told herself. It was like a nightmare. And there was worse to come.

Talking to Leon as he mixed drinks, Talia saw the shining dark head of the one woman in the world she actually hated—Alex's mistress, Joanna Dominic.

She wanted to run, and had actually turned on her heel when Leon spotted her.

'Talia! Come in. What will you have to drink?' He moved towards her, smiling, and she knew that it was too late. She was trapped.

CHAPTER FIVE

SHE could not remember a more embarrassing, terrifying moment. The conversation seemed to stop dead, the sudden silence was brittle and menacing. She could feel the hot colour staining her cheeks and she kept her head down, unable to meet the eyes she could feel on her face.

'Let me introduce you,' said Leon. He was jovial, putting her sudden silence down to shyness.

'We've already met.' Alex's low sardonic voice was too near and she looked up quickly. He was standing beside her, staring down at her with unfathomable grey eyes. She had no idea what he was thinking, he did not seem in the least surprised to find her here.

'Hello, Alex,' she managed in a small, almost steady voice.

'Well, what a coincidence!' Leon looked pleased, unaware of the terrible tension in her.

'Indeed.' Alex smiled slightly, still watching her, somehow giving the impression that it had nothing at all to do with coincidence.

She smiled at Joanna Dominic, even though it almost killed her.

'Hello, Miss Dominic.' The other girl looked stunning in red silk that contrasted starkly with her dark hair and tanned skin.

'Hello,' Joanna Dominic replied without interest, her eyes easy to read. She was angry, Talia realised with some satisfaction, angry and very surprised. But why should that be? Joanna Dominic had always had the upper hand, had always been able to defeat Talia.

78

And she had Alex, that much was still painfully obvious.

Luckily Alicia diverted Alex's attention at that moment and Talia followed Leon over to the drinks cabinet.

'Now, what shall I fix you?'

'A large whisky, please,' she replied, without hesitation.

Leon's brows rose, a silent question, but he poured out a large measure of Scotch and handed it to her. She sipped it almost eagerly, her mind paralysed.

'How long have you known Alex?' Leon asked curiously, perhaps sensing something in her.

'Some years now.' She was deliberately noncommittal. 'How about you?'

'Oh, we've been friends for many years.' He took her arm. 'Let's sit down.'

Talia managed to manoeuvre herself next to Jake, so that he sat between her, Leon and Joanna Dominic. Alex sat opposite to her now, still chatting to Alicia, and Talia found her eyes drawn to him.

He looked magnificent, hard and cool and powerful, his dark hair neatly brushed back from his tanned face, over-long, touching the collar of his velvet dinner jacket. She watched him smile, her heart turning over, even though he wasn't smiling at her, his grey eyes warm with that lazy charm she remembered so well.

She knew this mood, when he was relaxed, his hard body indolent, his mouth twisting with easy amusement. She knew that behind it all his shrewd, brilliant mind was working, assessing, understanding, effortlessly dissecting people and their motives.

He was a stranger, she realised, even though her memories were so haunting, so strong. The man who sat opposite her now wore that polished air of success, of wealth, of self-assurance and awareness. His narrowed eyes held a cool masculine sexuality that left most women reeling. She could see the effect he was having on Alicia and she knew he wasn't even trying.

She stared into the amber liquid in her glass. Alex's son lay sleeping upstairs in her room, and Alex had no knowledge of his existence.

Alicia, Leon and Jake all knew. How could she hope to keep Matty a secret from Alex after tonight? She swallowed, her body rigid with fear, her fingers clenched around the glass she held. One careless word, that was all it needed. A fine perspiration beaded her forehead. She wanted to run. Every instinct screamed for her to escape. This dinner party tonight forecast disaster for her.

She glanced around the room, her eyes suddenly meeting Alex's, and their glances locked fiercely. Her breath caught in her throat.

His eyes were dark, very serious. She could read no expression whatsoever in those grey depths, and yet there was an awareness, a violent bitter emotion crackling between them. Talia lowered her eyes first, her cheeks running high with colour, her heart pounding. She turned to Jake, whose mood she could see had not improved since that morning and the difficult scene at breakfast, launching into light superficial chatter, aware that Alex still watched her.

She spent the whole of the meal in a nervous panic, only speaking when spoken to, just waiting for the moment when someone would mention Matty.

Mrs Rodale's food was delicious, but she pushed it around her plate as though it was sawdust.

As time wore on, she began to realise something. The quieter she kept, the less attention she attracted. Both Alicia and Joanna Dominic were dominating the conversation, and as far as they were concerned Talia did not exist. Neither had any intention of including her in the conversation. So she kept as silent as possible, unable to stop herself watching Alex from beneath her lashes, and as soon as the meal was over, when everybody drifted towards the lounge for coffee and brandy, she managed to slip away, lingering by the windows in the dining room, praying, *praying* that the evening would soon be over.

A slight noise behind her, a few moments later, betrayed that she was not alone, and she jerked her head round.

Alex was standing by the door, smoking idly, watching her with blank, narrowed eyes.

Talia took a deep shaky breath and turned back to the windows, hoping he would go away, knowing that he wouldn't.

She did not hear him move, but he was suddenly beside her, staring down at the vulnerable line of her profile.

'Please go away,' she said huskily. He ignored her, expelling a long stream of smoke from his nostrils.

'Why are you in here alone?' he queried expressionlessly.

She shrugged, moving an inch or two away, finding it hard to breathe when he was so close.

'I don't want any coffee.' She did not look at him.

'I like your dress,' he said softly. 'Black suits you.'

It suits my mood, she thought to herself, almost smiling.

'Do you have a cigarette?' she asked, not acknowledging the compliment.

He held out a gold case to her, watching her fingers trembling as she extracted a cigarette.

Their eyes met, Talia's veering away immediately, as he held out a lighter.

'Thank you.' She drew on the cigarette deeply, her body tense, achingly aware of him.

'Do you enjoy working for Leon?' The question sounded casual, but he was still watching her, and she turned on him in panic, frightened of his motives for asking. He was too clever. Did he already know?

'I don't want to talk to you, can't you see that? I want to be left alone. I'm sure you've been missed. Miss Dominic——' She broke off abruptly, angry at her own betrayal, her face flushing.

Alex smiled. 'Really, Talia, I could almost believe you're jealous,' he taunted, running a long careless finger down her cheek.

His touch shuddered through her and she backed away. 'Don't touch me,' she whispered, totally hostile, paling as she saw the tightening of his mouth. She heard him swearing under his breath.

'What in God's name is the matter with you?' His voice was cool and quiet, yet violently angry. 'Your eyes flash hatred, you jump like a frightened child every time I come near you—tell me why, Talia.'

'Why don't you just leave me alone?' she repeated stonily. 'Can't you take a hint?'

'I think you overestimate your subtlety.' There was an ironic edge to his voice and, sure that he was laughing at her, she whirled away, inexplicable tears welling up, blinding her vision.

At that very moment Jake appeared in the doorway of the dining room. His eyes sharpened on Talia's pale tense face, his voice embarrassed as though he felt he was intruding.

'Sorry, Talia, Matty's calling for you. I think he had a bad dream. Belle is with him, but he wants you.'

Talia closed her eyes. It was the moment she had been dreading, and she realised that her fear went back to when Matty was born. She had actually been afraid of this moment for over two years, and incredibly there was a weird quality of relief in her horror.

'I'll come up now,' she said quietly, not even glancing at Alex, her mind focusing on her son.

She ran upstairs quickly. He was sitting up in bed, his small face miserable and wet with tears. Belle was hovering, trying to comfort him. Talia took his strong little body into her arms and he clung to her as she gently rocked him. She sang to him, her voice high and pure, then when she felt him drooping sleepily, she laid him back against the pillows, staring at him, seeing Alex in every line of his child's face, her heart aching with love for him.

He was asleep now, so she tucked him in, leaving on the light and wandering into her small lounge.

She did not want to go downstairs again. By now Alex would know that she had a child. On the other hand, of course, she couldn't just disappear without even making an excuse.

She felt cold and numb and almost uncaring as she left the room and walked slowly downstairs. She owed Leon some courtesy, she would make her excuses to him and come straight back upstairs.

To her intense relief there was no sign of Alex as she went into the lounge. Alicia and Joanna Dominic were talking, Leon and Jake standing by the drinks cabinet laughing. She made her way towards the two men.

'How is he?' Jake asked immediately.

'Fine—asleep again.' She smiled at both of them. 'If you'll excuse me, I think I'll go to bed. I have rather a bad headache.'

She escaped as soon as she could, gritting her teeth as she said goodbye to Joanna Dominic, who was obviously bitchily pleased to see her go, so relieved as she closed the lounge doors behind her.

But her relief was shortlived. On reaching the bottom of the stairs, she suddenly found Alex blocking her way, his grey eyes hard, his mouth tight.

Talia looked into his closed face and her heart leapt into her throat at the violence emanating from him.

'Jake tells me you have a child,' he said furiously, getting straight to the point, eyes probing on her downturned face.

'And what business is that of yours?' Talia demanded flatly, filled with dread, prepared to fight if she had to.

His eyes glittered, scorching her. 'What the hell happened to your lover, Talia, the man who still makes you melt whenever you think of him? Did he abandon you? Is that why you have to work here?'

Talia stared at him, open-mouthed, convinced that one of them had gone mad. Then as she realised what he thought, she began to laugh, high and hysterically, relief and total amazement coursing through her veins. Alex had no idea that he was Matty's father, it had not even crossed his mind for a moment that he might be, and inexplicably, she hated him for that even though she should be desperately glad.

'Matty's father is a cold uncaring swine,' she said with a brittle smile. 'I don't want him.' Her dark eyes burned feverishly as she looked at him. 'Now, if you'll get out of my way. . . .'

'Talia——' He tried to detain her, his jaw clenching as he looked at her.

'Ah, there you are, Alex.' Alicia's sweet voice broke between them, her eyes scathing on Talia. 'Do come and join us.'

Talia was halfway up the stairs before Alicia had finished speaking and she did not look back.

Once in her rooms, she locked the door, something she had never done before, and sank wearily into a chair, covering her face with her hands, feeling more exhausted than she could ever remember feeling before, her mind repeatedly crawling back over the awful embarrassing incidents of the evening.

Alex now knew that she had a son. She had never imagined that he wouldn't suspect it was his. Stupid really, because there was no reason why he should. They had not seen each other for three years, after all. He couldn't know that there had been nobody else for her, that she had not even looked at another man.

Who had there been for him? Joanna Dominic, obviously, although Alex had not yet married her. Did she still work for him?

So many unanswered questions. She could still remember the first time she had met Miss Dominic, four weeks after Alex had left for South America. Alex had mentioned her before. She came from a rich family, the daughter of one of Alex's best friends, apparently highly trained for the job she did. The memories were flooding back again with the thought of South America. Those four weeks after he left had been the longest of her life. She had waited and waited for some communication from him. There had only been silence. There was hardly any news coming out of the tiny republic, but she still scanned the newspapers every day—just in case. He had promised to ring—he had *promised*.

As the weeks passed, she became more and more anxious, unable to sleep, depressed, mechanically doing her job every day when all she wanted to do was stay in bed and cry. Perhaps he was hurt, dead even— that horrifying thought was soon dismissed. She would have heard about that, surely.

She heard on the television news that fighting was still going on and that communications had been severely hit, press teams expelled.

When she looked back on that time, she could remember it so clearly, and yet she could hardly remember it at all.

The day she found out she was pregnant was tinged with an aching, miserable despair, and a crazy kind of happiness that she was carrying Alex's child. She had still been hopeful.

On impulse, she had written him a letter, needing to do something, needing to feel that she was in some kind of communication with him. She had not told him that she was pregnant—it was not the sort of thing she could do by letter—only that she loved him, urging him to take care of himself. She had telephoned his flat in Knightsbridge, trying to obtain the address of his company in South America. His housekeeper had been friendly and polite, suggesting Talia ring his London office and speak to his personal secretary

His secretary had been out when she rang, and knowing that she could pass the office block on her way home from work, Talia didn't leave a message.

She remembered Joanna Dominic at her desk, slim and beautiful with shiny black hair that swung around her perfect jawline. There was something in her manner right from the start, something superior and faintly amused that made Talia feel inferior, childish and very ordinary.

Joanna Dominic's thin eyebrows rose as Talia haltingly explained about the letter, then she smiled, holding out a slim polished hand.

'I'm sending a package of papers out to Alex tomorrow, by special delivery, so if you give me your ... letter, I'll put it in.'

Talia hesitated for a moment, not really liking to give her letter to this beautiful woman, but then she handed it over with a slight shrug.

'Thank you.' There was nothing else she could do without seeming stupid. She watched Joanna Dominic's long fingers curling round the envelope and shivered.

'How long have you known Alex?' The beautiful secretary watched Talia's eyes melting, giving her away, even though her answer was not particularly forthcoming.

Talia returned to her flat feeling sure that Alex would contact her as soon as he received her letter. Almost two weeks passed and she heard nothing. She was working away at her desk one grey Monday morning when Joanna Dominic drifted in.

'I have an appointment with Mark,' she said coolly, and while Talia was ringing through to Mark's office, she pulled an envelope out of her briefcase. 'This telex came for you. It's from Alex,' she said with a saccharine smile. She handed it over and disappeared into Mark's office on a cloud of French perfume.

Talia could remember her hands trembling violently as she ripped open the envelope, her heart bursting with happiness. She had waited so long to hear from him. So long.

But her face paled as she read the telex, the shock making her stomach cramp with sickness. She read it again and again, unable to believe it, convinced she must be dreaming.

Brief and to the point, he stated that he would be in South America longer than expected. What they had had together had been good while it lasted, but as far as he was concerned it was over. It was blunt, almost brutal and cowardly—he did not even have the courage to tell her face to face.

Joanna Dominic's voice drifted from Mark's office, low, laughing, and Talia's face burned with humiliation. Joanna Dominic knew what the telex said. No wonder she had been so amused!

Talia wanted to run from the office, but a strange angry pride had stiffened her back as the office door swung open ten minutes later. She tried to keep her eyes blank as Joanna Dominic approached her desk, and looking at Alex's secretary, Talia had hated her at that moment.

Joanna Dominic's eyes were catlike, almost malicious. 'Bad news, darling?' She perched herself elegantly on the edge of the desk.

'Don't you know?' Talia tried to be cool, shock still holding her in its paralysed grip.

Joanna Dominic ignored that. 'Chalk it down to experience,' she suggested with a genuinely amused smile. 'Alex is very fickle—a man like that can afford to be.' Her eyes flicked over Talia, expression dismissive. 'Girls like you are ten a penny—you ought to be thankful for what you had from him.'

Her smile was knowledgeable as though she had inside information on every moment Talia had spent with Alex.

'How dare you!' Talia gasped, able to believe in her distraught state that Alex *had* talked about her to this beautiful woman who was his secretary—and what else?

Joanna Dominic shrugged. 'Oh, come on, you're not the first and I don't suppose you'll be the last. I can put up with it, because he always comes back to me.' Her pale eyes glittered with possession, and Talia felt sick. This woman was Alex's mistress and she was spelling out her warning for Talia to stay away.

'Just get out of here.' She lowered her head, suddenly weary, unable to cope with any more bad news.

'Really, darling, if Mark could hear you now!' Joanna Dominic's mouth tightened as she slid off the desk, and moved slowly to the door. 'And I wouldn't advise you to try and get in touch with Alex again,' she said over her shoulder. 'He's let you down fairly easily, but he doesn't take kindly to being pestered.'

Talia closed her eyes waiting for the bang of the door closing, and did not look up until she was sure the woman had gone.

Then she realised that her fists were clenched at her sides, her body rigid with tension, the breath caught in her lungs. Her thoughts were screaming in circles—there was so much pain inside her. Her whole life seemed ruined and it had only taken Joanna Dominic half an hour.

She didn't know how long she sat there, just staring into space, but when Mark dashed from his office some time later, on his way to a meeting, he took one look at her and put her in a taxi home.

The following weeks had been a nightmare. She threw the telex away, the message already burned into her brain. She wanted it destroyed. All this time she had been thinking of him, longing for him, hoping perhaps that there was some future for them when he returned, and he had probably not even spared her a thought. Her letter had no doubt been an unwelcome reminder of something he had thought left far behind.

She wouldn't have thought him so cruel, so cowardly, which all went to show how little she had really known him. In all the time they had spent together, he had always urged her to talk about herself, she had never found out very much about him at all.

For him it had been a brief affair—'good while it lasted'. Bitterness welled up inside her, because for her it had been love, for the very first time, and definitely the last. For her, it was not so easy to extricate herself; she was carrying his child. Alex did not give a damn, he only wanted to be free of her. And worse than all that was the knowledge that he was Joanna Dominic's lover, had been all the while, would continue to be. Joanna Dominic seemed to know all about Talia. Alex must have told her, and his betrayal destroyed her.

Her pregnancy was nine months of sheer hell. As well as the practical problems of somewhere to live and money to live on, there had always been that desolation inside her, the knowledge that Alex did not care, had never cared, had used her, surely knowing that she was falling in love with him.

She despised her own weakness because in her heart she still expected a miracle, still expected that he would get in touch with her again. She despised her own lack of judgment and she despised him.

Yet in the pain of Matty's birth, she cried out for Alex over and over again, a desperate humiliation, and even though she was determined to have the baby adopted, wanting nothing of the past or Alex in her life, when the child was put into her arms, she knew she could never give him up. She loved him as much as she had loved Alex. It seemed a final defeat.

Three months later, in a desperate, resentful mood, something drove her to go and see Alex. However much she pretended to hate him, her love refused to die, and although she battled against it, she knew in her heart that he had the right to know that he had a son. She wanted nothing from him—nothing at all.

She was frightened to death as she entered the tall office block, her heart pounding so fast she was afraid it would burst. She didn't know what was driving her on, when all she wanted to do was run like the wind.

She took the lift to the top floor and the executive suites, sickness clawing in her stomach, and walked towards Alex's offices.

A glass door barred her way and what she saw through it stopped her dead in her tracks, shrinking her against the wall.

Beyond the glass door, in the large brightly-lit outer

office, two figures stood passionately entwined. Alex and Joanna Dominic.

Talia turned on her heel and ran. Any stupid lingering doubts she might have had were destroyed. She had seen them together. Joanna Dominic had been telling the truth, and Talia needed no further proof.

She did not remember getting back to the house, she remembered only a haze of pain. A week later she had left for France and new employment, and she had not seen Alex again for over two years. . . .

She had been crying, the tears drying on her face, she realised, as her thoughts brought her back to the present. Those years had hurt her, more than she cared to admit, but seeing Alex again, seeing him wherever she went, it seemed, hurt more because of the terrible confusion it brought. Damn him, damn him, damn him! She got to her feet and lit a cigarette, moving restlessly across the room towards the windows.

Outside the night was bright, the moon high. The long windows were open and below she could hear voices. Joanna Dominic and Alex were leaving. Talia's eyes were drawn to him as he slammed shut the passenger door of the low black car and walked indolently round to the driver's seat. He smiled at Alicia and Leon, talking, though she could not catch the words, and then, as though sensing he was being watched, he raised his head and saw her in the upstairs window.

Their eyes met and Talia immediately backed away trembling, pulling closed the heavy curtains, hearing the car below roaring into life.

She hardly slept at all that night; her brief snatches of sleep were fitful, haunted by nightmare, and consequently she felt weary and depressed the following morning.

It was another beautifully cloudless day, but she could not muster up any enthusiasm for it as she sipped her breakfast coffee in tired silence, forcing herself not to take out her foul mood on Matty. Frowning as he watched her, Jake offered to take Matty and Belle swimming in the pool.

Talia thanked him, feeling both relieved and guilty because it was her job to look after the children, but today she felt as though she could not cope. Everything was beyond her, that old nameless defeat she had thought conquered lay on her mind like cold mist.

She spent the morning in her rooms, unable to concentrate her mind on any of the hundred and one things she ought to be doing. She was so restless, so tired.

On her way down to lunch, Alicia caught her at the bottom of the stairs.

'Are you feeling better?' the beautiful older woman asked politely, her eyes skimming over Talia's tight jeans and sleeveless green blouse.

'Yes, thank you.' She had disappeared after breakfast pleading a bad headache.

'Good. I'd like to have a word with you before lunch.' Alicia smiled, indicating the lounge.

'Of course.' Talia ran a careless hand through her red hair. She had the distinct feeling that this little chat would not be to her advantage.

'Would you like a drink?' Alicia moved with the careful grace of a top model.

'Sherry, please.'

Alicia poured two and seated herself opposite Talia.

'I wanted to see you before Leon got back,' she began, getting immediately to the point.

Talia sipped her drink in silence; she could almost guess what was coming next. It was all she needed.

'Leon's very pleased with the job you've been doing here, and of course I agree with him. The children are very fond of you—Jake to an almost ridiculous degree.' Alicia paused, still smiling, lighting a long cigarette. 'I know Leon has guaranteed your job here for as long as you want it, but. . . .' There was a delicate silence as though she was unsure how to continue.

'You'd like me to start looking for something else?' Talia hazarded drily.

In a way, she could see Alicia's point of view. She wanted the house and the family to herself. She was not getting any younger. Insecurity hung round her when confronted with Talia's youth. Talia was a threat, however small, to the new start she was trying to build.

'Well . . . yes, if you could keep your eyes open. Obviously I'm not suggesting you rush into just any job. . . .' Alicia's voice trailed off, her meaning clear. 'The thing is, you see, now that I'm back—well, to put it bluntly, you're superfluous. I can look after the children.'

Talia finished her sherry and stood up. She did not want to argue. 'I'll start looking right away,' she promised tonelessly.

It was not going to be easy and it would require energy and hope she felt sure she did not have. It had all been too good to be true, she realised now, this job, Leon's friendship. She had just walked into it, and nothing ever came that easy.

'I'm so glad you understand.' Alicia rose too, smoothing down the bright cotton of her dress. Talia smiled, suddenly aware that Alicia felt guilty, and left the room in search of Matty.

Later that afternoon, when the house was empty, Talia sat in the sun and wondered what on earth she would do, halfheartedly playing with Matty as she wrestled with her problems and came up with no practical solutions.

Matty, sensing her lack of involvement, began to lose interest in the game. 'I'm thirsty,' he said belligerently, his dark head on one side as he stared at her, grey eyes accusing.

'Well then, let's go inside and get some milk, shall we?' she suggested brightly, tired of thinking and worrying.

'Carry me, Mummy!' Matty demanded guilelessly.

Talia smiled at him and lifted him into her arms, holding his strong little body tightly.

He chuckled with delight as they made their way round the side of the house to the kitchen door, suddenly coming face to face with the very last person Talia wanted to see. Alex.

CHAPTER SIX

TALIA stared at him in blank horror, absently noting how attractive he looked in tight jeans that clung to his lean hips and a green shirt open at the neck. This just wasn't her day, she thought hysterically. Fate was certainly working against her.

Matty had become quiet and serious in her arms, gazing with interest at Alex, who was standing perfectly still, his grey eyes moving slowly from Talia to the child she held so close to her. Talia felt faint, a chill creeping over her as she looked into Alex's expressionless face.

'Dear God,' he said quietly, shaking his head in disbelief, the relentless sunlight glinting in his dark hair.

Talia hardly heard him. She gently lowered Matty to his feet; she couldn't hold him any longer, he was suddenly too heavy for her. She couldn't even stand up properly herself, the ground was moving beneath her feet. She heard Matty crying out her name as she fell into blackness.

When she opened her eyes again, she was inside the house, in the lounge, lying on one of the long couches, with no idea of how she had got here. Alex stood over her, his face taut, an angry mask, and Matty stood at his side, clutching his hand and staring up at her with wide tearful eyes.

'How are you feeling?' Alex asked tersely.

'Better. Could ... could I have some water?' she whispered, feeling the dryness in her mouth.

Alex nodded. 'Do you want a doctor?' His curiously blank eyes burned down into hers.

'No . . . no. . . . I fainted, that's all—probably too much sun.' She felt very nervous, almost frightened as she stared back at him. He was so tall and strong and hard.

'Mummy. . . .' Matty's mouth wobbled as he spoke her name and she sat up, holding out her arms to him, her face gentle with love. He rushed into her arms, burying his face against her breasts.

'It's all right now, my darling,' she murmured as she comforted him. He was reassured quickly, and turned back to gaze at Alex, his eyes wide and wondering as though he knew that this tall dark man was a part of him.

'We have to talk,' Alex said quietly, as he handed her a glass of water.

Talia stiffened. 'Talk?' she repeated nervously. 'About what?'

'For God's sake, Talia——!' There was a harsh violent edge to his voice. His body was rigid with tense control.

'Not while Matty is here,' she cut in desperately.

Alex shrugged, his face implacable. 'As you wish—but we're going to talk sooner or later, whether you like it or not.' She felt the sheer force of his personality, of his presence, and she felt that terrible anger inside him. Was he deliberately trying to frighten her? What the hell did he want anyway?

She was suddenly irritated by his arrogance. 'You have no right to barge in here and tell me what I have to do,' she said with shaky defiance.

'I have every right.' Alex's dark glance slid significantly to the child beside her, his eyes darkening as he stared at the little boy.

'Just go away and leave us alone,' she said stonily, hugging Matty tighter against her body.

'It's too late for that.' His voice was very cool,

though she knew that angry violence still burned inside him.

'Why is it too late?' she demanded recklessly, only wanting him to go. 'It's never been too late before. You didn't give a damn before today—what's changed your mind?'

'You're not a child, Talia, don't act like one,' Alex bit back coldly.

'Why don't you go to hell!' she snapped, very angry herself now. She didn't know how he had the gall to be talking as he was. As far as she was concerned nothing—absolutely nothing—had changed. They had nothing to talk about.

He stared at her, his mouth tight, and she heard him swearing with violent softness.

'Go away,' she repeated coldly, as the door suddenly opened and Jake appeared.

'I heard voices,' he said, looking at Talia. 'Are you okay?'

'She's fine,' Alex cut in smoothly. Talia opened her mouth to protest that she could answer for herself, then shut it again. She did not want a row in front of Jake, and especially not in front of Matty.

'Oh ... oh, all right.' Jake looked distinctly uncomfortable, a dull red flush along his cheekbones as he looked from Alex to Talia.

'Would you do me a favour, Jake?' Alex suddenly smiled at the young man. Turning on his charm, Talia thought bitterly, as she watched Jake responding.

'Sure, what is it?'

'Would you give Matty a drink of milk, take him into the garden for a while? Talia and I have to talk.'

'Yes, of course.' Jake's eyes questioned Talia in silence, as he moved to take Matty's small hand.

Talia smiled weakly in consent, unable to talk, then watched as Matty and Jake disappeared, the door closing quietly behind them, shutting her in alone with Alex.

She felt a ridiculous urge to call Jake back, beg him not to leave her, but she bit her lip and let him go.

'Very sensible,' Alex drawled, reading her mind, watching the betraying colour staining her cheeks.

'Let's leave Jake out of this, shall we?' she said angrily.

Alex smiled. 'Finding his infatuation a little hard to handle?' he queried softly.

'He's not——' She stopped abruptly. Where was the point in lying? She knew very well that Jake was infatuated with her. Everybody knew—Leon, Rick, Alicia—and Alex had noticed it immediately.

'I haven't encouraged him, if that's what you think,' she said stiffly, wondering why she was making excuses.

'I don't think about it at all.' His voice was amused, mocking. 'Cigarette?' She nodded, gritting her teeth. That slight smile still curved his firm mouth as he lit her cigarette and then his own, and Talia longed to slap it from his lean face.

She sat in stony silence, watching him covertly as he moved indolently across the room, his wide shoulders tense, as he stared out through the long open windows. From outside in the garden she could hear voices, Jake and Matty. Jake singing in a loud crazy voice, Matty laughing with delight, shouting.

Alex watched them as he smoked. 'Why the hell didn't you tell me?' he demanded harshly, not turning to look at her. Had she not known better she might have thought she heard pain in his voice.

'What makes you so damned sure he's . . . he's your son?' she retorted tremulously, furious because she felt so guilty. He made her feel guilty.

Alex turned then, his grey eyes destroying her.

'Let's not play games, Talia, for God's sake. Matty is my son, I knew that as soon as I saw him——' He broke off, raking a hand through his dark hair, his eyes shadowed. 'And all this time, all these years, not so much as a bloody word from you!'

'What did you expect?' she flared angrily. 'I'd already made a fool of myself, was I supposed to carry on doing the same thing over and over again?'

Alex's eyes narrowed on her flushed face. 'And what the hell is that supposed to mean?'

'What do you think?' she almost shouted. 'I can imagine your reaction if I'd come to you and told you I was pregnant. How inconvenient that would have been! What would you have done, Alex? Told me to get rid of it? Given me money?' She knew she was being cruelly unfair, but she was too hurt, too angry to check her words.

Alex's body stiffened as she shouted her insults, his jaw clenching. He moved with lightning speed across the room, hauling her to her feet with hands that bruised her skin, shaking her until her body felt limp, her hair in tousled disorder around her flushed face.

'You stupid little bitch!' he grated, almost beyond control. Their eyes met, hers defiant and fearful, his narrowed, bleak with anger, and the contact was explosive, a dizzying tension clashing between them, a raw electricity that burned them both.

Talia instinctively backed away, breaking the eye contact, wrenching herself from his hands and moving quickly, putting distance between them across the room.

She heard Alex sigh heavily. 'You really thought that?' he asked coolly, and from his voice it was difficult to believe that he was angry.

'It was perfectly clear that your interest lay elsewhere,' she retorted stiffly, trying to control herself, realising that she was revealing her jealousy by making reference to Joanna Dominic.

'Was it?' Alex walked slowly towards her.

She watched him moving, watched his cool powerful grace, and backed away, frightened. If this topic of conversation continued she was going to find herself in deep water.

'Tell me.' His voice was cold, almost taunting.

Talia shook her head. 'Alex, please! Our ... our relationship was over, I didn't want you any more than you wanted me.' She stumbled over the painful lies. 'I didn't even want the baby until I saw him ... and ... and after that, I wanted to provide for him myself. I didn't need you then, and I don't need you now.' She dared to glance up at him, swallowing nervously. She wondered at the truth of her harsh words. There was pride, of course. She could hardly let him know that it had almost destroyed her when she received that careless telex. He would never know that. The other emotions raging inside her were complex and confusing. But this was no time to analyse, to think everything out rationally. This was a fight and there were no rules.

'You may not need me,' Alex said expressionlessly, 'but that child out there, my child, needs a father.' Talia glared at him, hating him because she knew in her heart that he was right. It was something she had known for a long time, something that worried her almost constantly.

'Why are you suddenly so concerned? You never have been before.'

'Dammit, I didn't know he existed before today—I could kill you for that!' His cynical eyes held hers and she knew he was remembering what she had said to him the night before: 'Matty's father is a cold uncaring swine.'

'Alex, please. . . .' Her dark eyes begged, for what she was not certain.

'I want him, Talia.' He did not bother to disguise his bitter determination.

She shook her head. 'You can't take him away from me!' she said fearfully, suddenly realising that he would go to any lengths to get what he wanted. 'You can't!'

'Do you want to fight it out in court?' He was implacable, as cold as ice. 'You wouldn't stand a chance.'

'I can give Matty everything he needs,' she whispered in horror.

'He needs a father.' Alex lit another cigarette with easy grace.

'So, I'll get married,' she retorted wildly. 'Believe me, I'll do anything to keep him!'

Alex's dark brows rose. 'Do you have anybody in mind?'

'Mind your own damned business!'

'There's nobody in your life,' he said evenly. 'I've made it my business to find that out. No boy-friend, no lover, nobody.

'Leon will help me.'

'Leon is already married,' he reminded her with a cold smile of amusement. 'And I doubt the lovely Alicia would take kindly to that idea. In fact, I'm surprised she's tolerated your presence here for so long.'

Talia closed her eyes, a feeling of lonely isolation washing over her. 'You bastard,' she said with quiet poison. He did not care how alone she was. He did not care that he was hurting her.

Alex's face tautened, his grey eyes very blank. 'I want my son. You have a choice—either you hand him over to me, or you marry me. I intend to have him, I'm telling you that now.'

His unexpected proposal shocked her to the core. Her heart began to pound deafeningly. 'Marry you?' Her voice was high, the words tumbling over themselves. 'You've got to be joking! I know what kind of a person you are, and I wouldn't marry you if you were the very last person on earth!'

Alex smiled slightly. 'I'd think very carefully about refusing, if I were you. After all, you have to consider Matty. I'm offering him wealth, security and everything else a child needs, including his natural father. Would you deny him all that?'

His cool words got to her, cutting her to ribbons inside.

'You're despicable,' she spat at him. 'I hate you!'

'Because I'm right?' The grey eyes were genuinely amused.

'Because you put me in an impossible position. Either I marry a man I hate, or I lose my son.' She could feel the tears of self-pity burning in her eyes.

'Do you really hate me so much, Talia?' His voice was mocking, but his eyes were deadly serious.

'After what you did, yes, I hate you,' she said emphatically.

'What did I do?' His voice was lazy, but she sensed the steel behind it. She was silent.

'Tell me,' he persisted. 'Let's get to the bottom of all this bitterness.'

'You used me—you never gave a damn.'

'No, it wasn't like that, it was never like that, I——'

'Well, what does it matter anyway? It's all in the past now,' she cut in quickly. She didn't think she would be able to stand it if he started talking about what they had once shared.

'And for some crazy reason you're so cold and bitter, you're prepared to deny your son his rights,' Alex bit out harshly.

Talia dashed a tear from her cheek with trembling angry fingers. She was trying to think clearly, but he was running her mind round in circles.

'Why have you asked me to marry you anyway? You could have Matty, you've said so yourself. You could take him away from me,' she said in a high shaking voice.

'I haven't asked you for any pleasure I'd get from seeing you going through hell being married to me, I can assure you,' he taunted softly. 'I have no wish to marry a woman who so obviously hates my guts—although it might be interesting to try and change your mind.' His narrowed eyes slid insolently down her body, in an intimate appraisal that stripped away every stitch of clothing.

Talia blushed brightly. 'Why, then?' she demanded huskily.

'Matty loves you, you love him. I don't want to take him away from you, despite what you think. I'll only do it if I have to,' he told her in that cool expressionless voice that gave her absolutely no clue as to what was going on inside his head.

'I see.' She didn't mean to sound sarcastic, but she knew it sounded that way, because Alex swore, his eyes becoming even bleaker as he watched her.

'For the love of God, you stubborn child, will it really be so awful? It's written in your face, burning in your eyes, how you've had to struggle these past three years. I'm offering you and Matty security for life. You can rest assured, it's him that I want, not you.'

For some reason, a totally inexplicable reason, his words hurt her. What on earth was the matter with her? She was *glad* he did not want her. 'Marrying you would solve one set of problems, I agree, but it would leave me with another set, just as bad but different, don't you see that?'

Alex was silent, his gaze steady, unwavering.

Talia looked into his lean dark face, her eyes moving slowly over the familiar, fiercely attractive features. The very thought of becoming his wife frightened her to death, set her stomach churning with alarm. There was no reason for it, she thought wearily. He had made it perfectly clear that he didn't want her, only Matty, and if she thought about it from Matty's point of view. . . .

'I'll have to think about it,' she said worriedly.

Alex nodded. 'Very well. I'll come back tomorrow, about the same time.' He was still angry.

'Tomorrow?' she asked in panic.

'Tomorrow,' he repeated, and moved towards her, reaching out his hand and running a lean finger down her cheek. 'You've already made up your mind.'

Talia took a shaky step back, his touch shrivelling her. Had she? She hated his calm certainty.

'I could run away. I could take Matty and go tonight.' It was a last desperate defiance. He thought he knew her so well.

'I'd find you,' he replied with a cool smile. 'Besides, you won't run, you're too honourable.'

'You don't know me at all,' she flashed. He was so knowledgeable, so perceptive.

'I know the woman behind the wall of ice,' he said softly, his voice deep with meaning.

'A person changes a lot in three years,' she told him flatly. 'And if I do marry you—*if*, I hope I can make your life a misery, I hope you suffer as I——' She stopped, biting her lip savagely.

'Revenge?' Alex queried mockingly. 'For what? What goes on in that mind of yours?'

'You'll never know,' she retorted. Alex smiled, his eyes glimmering with a strange tenderness. Taking her by surprise, he suddenly bent his head and touched his mouth to her forehead. Then he turned and walked towards the door.

'I'll see you tomorrow.'

Talia was silent, shocked by that gentle kiss, then she gritted her teeth, aching to throw something at him. She couldn't, of course, because everything in the room belonged to Alicia and Leon.

He turned in the doorway, his mouth amused. 'Don't bother to see me out, I can find my own way.'

'Oh, you . . . you. . . .' Before she could think of anything suitably vitriolic, the door was quietly closing and she could hear his soft laughter mocking her.

She walked over to the windows, her arms wrapped protectively around her body, feeling the shock of the past half hour wearing off. Throughout their entire conversation her brain had been working mechanically, and it was just sinking in that Alex had asked her to marry him.

She watched Matty playing a crazy kind of football with Jake and her eyes filled with desperate tears. What would she do? What choice did she have? It was all so damned unfair!

Alex had seen Matty for the first time today. He thought he could just walk in and take over. Alex always got what he wanted—that thought ran through her mind as she considered refusing him.

If it did go to court, surely she would win? The slight nagging doubt made it impossible to even contemplate. She couldn't take any chances on losing Matty. And there was absolutely no doubt that Matty needed Alex—that would become more and more apparent as he got older. If she thought of Matty's needs she would marry Alex, there was nothing else she could do.

But what about me? she thought dully. Why should

I have to marry a man I hate? Hate—the word rang in her mind. Did she hate Alex? Her feelings were utterly confused. She had certainly tried her hardest to hate him, but whether or not she had succeeded, she couldn't tell.

She realised that apart from Matty, her life was empty. There was no man in the world who cared for her, and if she was honest, it couldn't be any less empty if she married Alex. If she did not love him, surely he could not hurt her. It was not as though she had any particular hopes or plans for the future, in fact she had the feeling that she would never fall in love again.

She put a hand over her eyes and began to cry. Self-pity, she told herself sternly, but that didn't stop the tears. She had never felt so desolate or alone before in her life.

She cried until she felt exhausted, her tears drying, and strangely, she felt calmer and more in control as she blew her nose. What did it matter anyway where she lived, who she lived with?

Alex was right, damn him; she had created an impenetrable barrier of ice between herself and the world. All she had was Matty, and she had to put his happiness before her own. Alex had won, but he would get no satisfaction from her, she thought bitterly, no satisfaction whatsoever.

She sat wrestling with her thoughts until late in the afternoon, until Leon walked in, loosening his tie with weary hands, obviously just back from the city.

'Hello,' he smiled. 'All alone?' Talia nodded, and his blue eyes sharpened on her tear-stained face. 'What's wrong?'

She was silent. She did not want to bore Leon with her problems. 'Do you want a drink?' he asked, moving towards the cabinet. 'I surely need one, I've had one hell of a day.'

'A small Scotch would be nice,' she managed quietly.

'Right.' He fixed the drinks and sat down. 'Now, tell me what's wrong.'

Talia looked into his face and saw kindness and concern, realising what a true friend he was. 'Alex came this afternoon,' she revealed, staring down at the ice in her glass.

'He's Matty's father, isn't he?'

Talia's eyes widened. 'How did you know?'

Leon shrugged. 'It's obvious. They're as alike as two peas in a pod. I don't know why I didn't realise before last night.'

'Yes, I suppose they are alike.' Her voice was dull.

'Does he know about Matty?'

Talia nodded. 'He wants me to marry him.'

'Hey, that's great news!' Leon's face split in a broad grin.

'Is it?' She wished she could share even a tiny portion of his enthusiasm. Instead she felt cold, numb, almost uncaring.

'You don't want to marry him?'

'What I want is irrelevant. Alex wants Matty, so he's prepared to take me as well. I suppose I ought to be thankful for that small mercy.' She was icy with sarcasm.

'No, you must have it wrong.' Leon leaned forward in his chair, his expression serious. 'From what I picked up last night, I'm sure Alex cares for you.'

Talia smiled sadly. Leon was trying to reassure her. She felt a rush of affection for him. She would not tell him of the chat she'd had with Alicia before lunch. She didn't want to cause trouble. Marrying Alex would sort out that problem too. There would be no need to look for another job. If she looked at it from a purely practical angle, she was getting a good deal; at least the exhausting struggle would be taken out of her everyday life.

'You don't believe me, do you?' Leon swallowed back his whisky in one long mouthful.

'If you want me to be honest, no, I don't.'

'He asked a lot of questions about you last night. I don't know what happened between you two, but I'd stake practically anything on the fact that he cares, with or without Matty.'

'Leon——' The colour was rising in her cheeks and for some ridiculous reason, she felt embarrassed.

'No, listen to me, Talia. I've known Alex for a long time now. He's not an easy guy to get to know, and over the past few years there's been a kind of bitterness inside him. He may seem changed, but underneath it all he really cares about people—hell, much more than I do. You know that.'

'Yes, I suppose I do,' she admitted grudgingly.

'Well, remember that when you're deciding what to do.'

'I've already decided,' she told him, swigging back her whisky.

'And?'

'I'm going to marry him.' There was a flat defeat in her voice.

Leon frowned. 'So miserable! Don't you love him?'

'No,' she answered quickly, emphatically. 'I'm trying to look on the whole thing as a business deal. I want to be purely mercenary about it—after all, there are no real feelings involved.' Her mouth was hard, but her sad dark eyes gave her away. 'Trouble is, I'm not succeeding very well.'

She felt like crying, but her eyes remained dry, her throat aching. The release of tears was long past.

'It's not in your nature,' Leon said with a smile. 'You're gentle, highly-strung and sensitive. I don't believe you have a mercenary bone in your body. You can't be what you're not.'

'I suppose not.' She sighed and got to her feet. 'I'd better go and find Matty.'

'Talia——' Leon halted her as she reached the door. 'Dammit, I feel so worried about you,' he admitted wryly.

'Don't worry, Leon, I'll get by. I'm stronger than you think.' She smiled confidently, wanting to reassure him.

'Alex will take good care of you,' he told her, honestly believing it. 'But if you ever need a friend——'

'I know—thank you.' Her smile grew naturally radiant as she looked at him. She wasn't so alone after all.

She found Matty sleeping in his room. She stared down at him, her heart contracting with love, knowing she had made the right decision. Matty deserved the world if she could give it to him. She would never let him down.

Strolling through the garden some hours later, hoping to work up some sort of an appetite for dinner, she suddenly saw Jake sitting at the side of the pool, his feet up on another chair.

She approached him silently, the soft grass muffling her footsteps. 'You're going to be late for dinner,' she teased, and his head jerked round, his smile strained.

'I don't care—I'm not hungry,' he said, shrugging his shoulders.

Talia sat down and looked at him. He looked miserable, his lean body hunched and tense, his sweet face doleful.

'Thanks for looking after Matty this afternoon,' she said brightly.

'That's okay.' He turned his face away.

'Do you want to be alone?'

He sighed. 'Alex Jordan—he's Matty's father.' It was almost an accusation.

'Yes, he is.'

'Are you two . . . well, are you. . . .?'

'I'm going to marry him,' Talia said gently. She hated to hurt him, but there was nothing else she could do.

'So you'll be leaving,' Jake said flatly.

'Yes, almost immediately.' There was no point in lying.

Jake was silent, and she felt awful. She had never encouraged him, yet she knew that he was a little in love with her. Her heart ached because she knew what it was like to be young and in love. She knew all about the hell of unrequited love. Suddenly he looked at her and she saw the pain in his dark blue eyes. 'I wish you didn't have to leave.'

'We can still be friends,' she promised.

'Can we?' He looked doubtful.

'Oh, Jake. . . .' Her slim shoulders lifted, her eyes unsure. 'I don't know what to say.'

He stood up abruptly, his lean body graceful, and pushed his long hair out of his face. 'I thought that——' He stopped. 'Well, I thought—oh, hell, forget it.' He bent forward and kissed her cheek, taking her by surprise, then he was gone, running into the darkness of the gardens.

Talia touched her cheek. It was the worst thing in the world, hurting another person. Her fingers were wet and she realised that she was crying again.

She was in her room next day when Alex arrived. Alicia knocked on the door.

'Alex Jordan is here to see you,' she said, her pale beautiful eyes sliding curiously over Talia, as though seeing her for the very first time. Leon must have told her, Talia thought, almost smiling.

'Thank you, I'll be down right away.'

'You are a dark horse,' said Alicia, making no move to go back downstairs. Her face was hard, and Talia stared at her, puzzled. Alicia had wanted her gone—yet now she looked distinctly put out.

'Am I?' she asked with a smile.

'Who would have thought? Alex Jordan—he's quite a catch for any girl.' Her eyes told Talia that for her to have caught him was nothing short of a miracle.

'Yes, I suppose he is,' Talia said uncaringly, and turned back into the room. She had no intention of letting Alicia third-degree her.

Alex was in the lounge, standing indolently by the windows, when Talia entered. He looked tall and strong and overpoweringly attractive in a dark pin-striped suit, expensively tailored to his magnificent physique. The formality of the suit lent him a remoteness that spoke of power and success, and made her heart pound deafeningly in her chest.

'Hello,' she managed through dry lips.

He turned slowly from the windows, his grey eyes unreadable as they slid over her, taking in her tight jeans and red tee-shirt, the dark circles under her eyes and her pale flawless skin, the fragility that gave away the fact that she had not slept the night before.

'Hello.' His mouth curved in a slight smile.

'Alicia asked me to ask you if you would like some coffee.' She relayed the message like a polite child.

'Yes, I'd like some coffee, but not if the price is Alicia's company,' he said drily.

'I don't know about that,' Talia said uncomfortably. 'Don't you like her?'

'I came to see you,' he smiled.

'Oh.' She was flustered by the warm charm of that smile.

The sun made the room very bright, the harsh light

accentuating the hard line of his jaw, the dark hollows beneath his cheekbones, it gave his skin a tanned, healthy sheen, it glinted in the blackness of his hair. He disturbed her.

'I'll see about the coffee, then.' She shot from the room like a scalded cat, hating him for the effect he had on her, hating herself for her response.

Fortunately there was no sign of Alicia. She made the coffee herself in the enormous kitchen, it being Mrs Rodale's morning off. I'll miss this place when I leave, she thought miserably as she waited for the percolator. It was the first place where she had felt really content since before Matty was born. Nothing lasted—that was a lesson she had learned very young. Even if Alex had not forced her hand, Alicia would have got rid of her, sooner or later.

She longed for some sort of permanence, some security. The coffee was ready all too soon and she carried it into the lounge feeling as though she was walking to the scaffold. Today she would tell Alex that she would marry him. From that moment on, he would take over her life. In a way it would be a relief to hand over the constant burden of responsibility, but it meant the end of her freedom.

'Where's Matty?' Alex asked, watching her as she set down the tray.

'Out with Jake and Vinnie,' she replied succinctly. 'I thought it better. . . . How do you like your coffee?' She knew very well how he took it, she remembered everything she had ever learned about him, but she was not about to let him know that.

'Black, no sugar.' His mouth twisted. He knew she remembered.

The silence stretched tautly between them, building up a tension that filled the room. They had nothing to say to each other, Talia realised in panic. Would it always be that way? How on earth would they be able to live together in such an atmosphere?

She knew that Alex was watching her. She did not look up, just gripped her coffee cup tightly, praying that her hands would stop trembling.

'Have you reached a decision?' His voice cut into the silence, strange and rough.

Talia took a deep breath, and finally looked up at him, her eyes wide, lovely and very scornful. 'Yes, I'll marry you, but I want to make it clear right from the start that I'm doing it for Matty and because I don't want you to take him away from me. I also want you to know that I don't like you very much and I think what you've done is—despicable!' She watched his eyes become cold and blank as she spoke, watched the slight stiffening of his body, with a strange satisfaction. Perhaps this time she really had pierced that thick skin, really had got to him. She hoped so.

'You make yourself very clear,' he said coolly, his voice bored and uncaring. 'And frankly, I'm not affected one way or the other by your opinion of me.'

'That's fine, then, isn't it?'

He smiled at her anger. 'Yes, it's fine,' he repeated softly.

Talia felt her teeth clenching together. 'When will I have to marry you?' she demanded stonily.

'In exactly one week's time,' Alex said clearly.

'*A week?*' It was too soon, and her panic showed on her face.

'There's no point in putting it off.'

He was so damned cool, she thought bitterly. All her own calmness, the numb, stony acceptance that she had thought would sustain her through this meeting, suddenly dissolved without trace, leaving her raw and aware and trembling violently.

She was shaking so badly that hot coffee spilled

from her cup, making her gasp with pain as it scalded her skin.

Alex was beside her in a split second, forcing her clenched fingers from the handle of the cup, producing a handkerchief from his pocket and mopping the spill from the leg of her jeans.

'Dear God, you're shaking like a leaf,' he muttered, frowning.

'Leave me alone,' she whispered shakily, his nearness, his concern, which she knew to be false making her heart beat hurriedly.

'Talia, listen to me——' His voice was low and very gentle, and she could not bear it.

'I'm all right,' she said loudly, cutting across him. 'And I don't want to listen to you. You've got what you came for, why don't you just go now?'

He stood up, his mouth tight. 'As you wish,' he said icily.

'As I wish?' she repeated hysterically. '*As I wish?* I must be mad to have agreed to all this!'

'Nevertheless, you have agreed, and you'll marry me one week from today!'

His eyes flicked over her once, cold and implacable, then he turned and walked from the room, leaving her alone and peversely wishing that he had not gone.

CHAPTER SEVEN

THE wedding was a very quiet affair. Incredibly, Alex had suggested a church wedding, but in horror Talia had insisted on a civil ceremony.

He was quite mad, she thought, when he offered her money to buy a dress. 'You'll need something special,' he had said coolly.

Talia had laughed, ignoring the tightening of his mouth. 'Why?' she had demanded scornfully. 'It's nothing more than a joke, a formality. I don't care what I wear.'

'But I do,' he had told her bleakly. 'And you'll buy something beautiful, something special. I'll come with you, if I have to.'

'Oh, very well, if you insist.' She had grudgingly taken the money, knowing that it was useless to argue.

'I do insist.' He had smiled then, his eyes dark with an angry tenderness that had trapped Talia's breath in her throat.

The engagement ring was another surprise. He had slipped it on to her finger, a single flawless diamond set in gold. It was beautiful, but it was a stamp of his possession and it frightened her.

'No,' she had said, staring up at him with blind eyes. Alex had not said a word, his eyes holding hers, silencing all her protests.

As instructed, she travelled up to London, leaving Matty in Mrs Rodale's capable care, and spent an afternoon scouring the shops. She had no idea what she was looking for, but kept on looking until she found something suitable. It was cream silk, a beautifully cut dress with a camisole style bodice, and a soft matching jacket. She examined her reflection in the fitting room mirror and smiled, knowing it was perfect.

It was wildly expensive, and usually she wouldn't have dreamed of buying something so extravagant, but, she reflected, as she sat in the taxi on the way back to the house, she was merely obeying Alex's orders. He obviously had money to burn.

The week had passed like a speeded-up film, as the wedding loomed nearer and nearer.

Talia had tried to keep her mind occupied, tried not to think what she was committing herself to. There was, after all, no turning back.

Leon and the rest of the family, even Alicia, probably because she wanted to see the back of her, had been wonderfully helpful, but Talia had been depressed. She had no courage or enthusiasm. She knew she ought to be sorting things out with Alex, details like where they would live, how they would live, but she was fully aware that he had everything in hand. No doubt he would tell her in his own good time, she thought dully. It was as though part of her refused to accept that she would be marrying him. By not knowing any details, it seemed less real, she could pretend that it was not happening.

Alex had taken her and Matty to the zoo one afternoon. It had been an order, but Talia had agreed without argument because it was important that Matty get to know his father.

She watched them together with an aching heart, Alex, tall and indolent, smiling, Matty, travelling on his shoulders, delighted, so like his father. They got on well. There had been a strange bond of under-standing between them right from the beginning, a friendship and affection, and Talia, although she hated herself for it, was jealous, terribly jealous. It was very difficult to share something so precious, especially with someone you didn't like very much.

Despite all that, the afternoon at the zoo had been a success. Alex had been warm and charming and she had found part of herself unwillingly responding to that charm. She had been relieved, though, when he dropped them back at the house. She had been able to carry Matty inside and shut the door on Alex.

She had so little time left, and she needed it for herself. She had told Alex that, the following day when he had telephoned and suggested another outing. He had been angry, very cold, and his sarcasm cut into her. She knew she was being awkward, but didn't she have the right to be, after all he had done? Then, before she had time to blink, it was her wedding day.

The ceremony passed very quickly, almost before she realised. She felt numb as Alex slid the gold band on to her finger. She did not look at him, but listened to his deep voice as he took his vows. It was totally unreal, she thought, as she sat next to him in his car, when it was all over. She was his wife. She shivered, and he turned his dark head, taking his eyes off the road for a second.

'Cold?' he queried expressionlessly.

Talia shook her head. 'Frightened,' she replied in a small voice.

'Of what? Of me?' His voice was mocking.

'Of what I've just done.'

Alex was silent and she absently watched his brown hands tightening on the wheel.

'Where are we going now?' she asked, not really interested, but worrying unnecessarily about Matty, who had been left in the capable hands of Mrs Craven, the housekeeper at Alex's Knightsbridge flat. She had liked Mrs Craven immediately, even though she was haunted by the memory of telephoning and asking her about Alex's company in South America. Mrs Craven had kind eyes and a soft laugh, and Talia felt that Matty was in very good hands.

'Wait and see,' Alex replied, with a faint smile.

It was her own fault, she supposed, for not bothering to ask him about the arrangements, for telling him to get on with them himself, but she felt a stab of irritation at his words.

'I'm tired,' she told him belligerently.

'Of course you're not,' he soothed, as though she was a fretful child.

She stared at his hard profile, at the firm warmth of his mouth, and shivered again.

'Alex——'

'Talia, be quiet. We're almost there.' His voice was amused, yet beneath it was a quality of tenderness that made her heart beat faster. What have I done? she asked herself desperately. What the hell have I done?

Alex had arranged a small wedding breakfast at the Ritz. Talia gasped with amazement when she saw everybody—Matty, clinging to Mrs Craven's hand, Kate, Alicia and Leon, and for some ridiculous reason she felt tears welling up in her eyes, a reaction, perhaps, to the icy coldness that had held her in its grip during the wedding ceremony.

Alex took her arm, and she tried to pull away, his casual touch searing through the thin silk of her jacket. His grip tightened bruisingly, and he looked down at her, his jaw clenching.

'For God's sake, try and look a little happier. This isn't a goddamned wake!'

Talia glared up at him. 'I don't feel happy.'

'And do you want all your friends to know that?' he muttered harshly.

'I don't care what they think,' she retorted, but she was lying. It was between Alex and herself. It was nobody else's business. So she smiled and drank champagne and chattered brightly, her mind blank underneath it all.

'Lovely party.' Kate suddenly appeared at her side. 'And you look beautiful.'

'Thanks.' Talia smiled for real at her friend. 'I'm glad you came. I had no idea about all this.' She spread her hands expressively.

'I know. Alex told me it was to be a surprise, when he invited me. That's quite a man you have there.' Kate was openly envious, and Talia watched Alex across the room. He was laughing, his grey eyes warm, faintly cynical. Her heart somersaulted.

'Yes, I think you're right,' she agreed in a soft voice.

She had told Kate about the wedding, of course, but something had held her back from telling her friend the whole story. Kate was ecstatic. She swore she had known all along that they would get together, ever since that night in the restaurant. Kate thought they were in love, and she was so happy for Talia and Matty. Talia knew that her friend would worry if she knew the truth. There was no point in worrying her when there was nothing she could do.

The party drifted on. Talia drank too much champagne and stayed near Matty. She was beginning to feel quite happy, lightheaded, smiling brilliantly at people who came and went, congratulating her, wishing her well for the future, enthusing over Matty and how much he looked like Alex.

Then Alex suddenly appeared by her side, his eyes narrowing as he took in her flushed drowsy face.

Talia smiled at him uncaringly. Their eyes met and he smiled back. 'I forgot to tell you before—you look very lovely.' His voice was husky, very low.

She flushed at the deep compliment. 'So do you.' She laughed breathlessly, all her aggression towards him, towards everybody and anybody, gone in a haze of champagne bubbles.

'You've been drinking far too much,' he told her with calm amusement.

'It gives the world a rosy sheen, it helps me to forget,' she replied, and the sentence ended on a hiccough.

'I think it's time we were leaving.'

'Are you afraid I'll make a fool of you?'

Alex shook his head, his mouth curving in a smile. 'No, of yourself.'

'Why isn't Joanna here?' she asked suddenly.

'She wasn't invited,' Alex replied, staring at her.

'Oh.' She was lost for words, surprised by his tact.

'Any more questions?' His mouth was indulgent.

'I'm so tired,' she whispered, swaying towards him. Lack of sleep during the past week was catching up on her, together with the delayed effect of the alcohol she had consumed. She felt exhausted, but when she closed her eyes, everything began to spin round and round.

The next thing she knew, she was in the car with Matty and Mrs Craven, speeding towards Alex's flat, and when they arrived, she found her legs so weak they wouldn't support her.

Alex swung her effortlessly into his arms and carried her to a cool dark bedroom.

'Matty——' she began worriedly.

'Mrs Craven will look after him—everything will be all right.' His low voice reassured her and she wrapped her pale arms around his neck, marvelling at his strength, wondering why his heartbeat speeded up as she nestled closer. She felt as though she was floating, almost unaware of Alex's hands moving gently, carefully removing her clothes.

All she wanted to do was sleep. Matty was safe and she had nothing to worry about.

'Lie down.' Alex's voice was rough. She did as she was told, the sheets soft and cool against her bare skin. She was asleep before he had pulled the covers over her. . . .

When she woke again, she thought it was dark. It felt late. She stretched lazily, hearing the faint hushed roar of the traffic outside, then opened her eyes, wondering where she was for a moment, and as she realised, her body seemed to cramp with pain.

A small lamp bathed a circle of the room in a rosy glow and Alex was sitting in a chair near the bed, reading a newspaper. As though sensing she had woken, he looked over at her. 'So you're awake at last.'

He smiled as she flushed brightly. Their eyes met and held. Talia looked away first.

'What . . . what time is it?' She struggled into a sitting position, pushing back her tousled hair, and as the silken covers fell away, realised that she was naked. Her hand fell from her head in shock. Alex was staring at her body, at her bared breasts, his eyes suddenly smoky and unsmiling. Her heart began to pound heavily and she pulled the sheet up under her chin, her fingers clenching convulsively.

'It's after eight.' His reply was cool, amused.

'Where's Matty?' she asked sharply. She could hardly believe she had slept the afternoon away.

'Mrs Craven put him to bed an hour ago. I told him you'd go and see him when you got up.'

He was still staring at her with those dark, heavy eyes, and she could feel her whole body responding to him, aching with a fierce warm desire she had thought long dead. She felt angry at such a response, she hated him, she could not possibly want him. It was the intimacy of the softly lit bedroom, the fact that they were alone.

'Where are my clothes?' she demanded in a cold little voice.

Alex lazily indicated another chair.

'Did you . . . was it you who . . .?' She swallowed, wondering why on earth she wanted to know.

'Yes, I undressed you,' he said calmly. 'You were in no state to do it yourself.'

Her face burned with embarrassment. Presumably it gave him some perverted satisfaction to embarrass her, to remind her that she had drunk far too much at the reception.

'Well, at least the champagne cheered me up. It helped me to forget this fiasco,' she said, her mouth a fierce defiant line.

Alex smiled. 'I could help you a whole lot more.' There was a husky mockery in his voice, leaving her in no doubt of his meaning.

'You couldn't help me at all!' she snapped back, trembling. 'Now, would you mind getting out of here while I get dressed?'

She sounded as though she was talking to a servant, and Alex's mouth tightened ominously. He stood up slowly, his movements angry, very graceful. He had removed his jacket and his tie and his waistcoat was unbuttoned. He looked powerful, indomitably male in the dim intimate light of the bedroom.

Talia felt her heart beating with fear and heat as he moved closer to the bed. His intentions were obvious. 'Go away,' she said in a voice that shook.

'You ought to know better than to provoke me, my love,' he murmured, staring down at her body, clearly visible beneath the thin sheet.

'Alex, please. . . .' Her throat ached with tension. She could see the raw desire, the anger in his grey eyes.

His mouth twisted. 'Oh, I can please you.' His voice was liquid, melting her bones. He reached for the sheet, jerking it from her fingers in one smooth movement.

She lay perfectly still, held by shock, as his brilliant gaze roamed slowly over her naked body.

'You're so beautiful,' he said softly. 'You were beautiful three years ago, but now you have the body of a woman. Your breasts are fuller, your hips more curved.' He reached down, his long fingers tracing the soft line of her shoulder. His touch shuddered through her, her body tautening, aching.

She knocked his hand away in panic. 'Don't touch me!' she spat furiously. I should move, she thought desperately, get off this bed, *now*. But she looked at Alex and lay still, held not by any physical restraint, but by the sheer force of his presence, his potent masculinity. She wanted him to want her, and that was a humiliating revelation.

'Don't touch me,' she repeated desperately. If she said it often enough, she might believe it to be what she wanted.

'Why the hell shouldn't I touch you?' he asked in a voice rough with emotion. 'You're my wife, I want you.'

He pinioned both her violent hands above her head with one of his.

'No. . . .' Her eyes widened with dawning realisation, dark, fevered.

'Did you really think it all came for free?' he asked harshly. 'With no price to pay? Your white body has haunted me for three years. You're mine, you've always been mine, but now it's legal and I can't believe you entered this marriage so damned naïvely.'

'You hate me,' she whispered, her heart clenching in pain.

Alex smiled, a rare tenderness glimmering in the depths of his eyes. 'No, Talia, I don't hate you. I want you, as you want me.'

'That's where you're wrong—I don't want you,' she said fiercely, and realised that she was lying. She wanted him, so badly. In the three years they had been apart she had never stopped wanting him; memories of his body against hers, his mouth against her skin, still haunted her day after day, night after night. Despite all she knew of him, despite all the pain he had caused her, she still wanted him.

'You're a liar,' he groaned softly. 'You tell me to go, but your eyes and your body beg me to stay. I'm only human, dammit.' He lowered his head very slowly, arching over her as she shivered as his mouth touched hers, gently at first, brushing her lips, parting them with hungry tender kisses. She told herself that she would show him no response. She *would not* show him how she wanted him. But as his mouth moved on hers, an all-encompassing desire rose up in her, consuming all her doubts, consuming everything, shaking her deeply with her need for him.

Her lips moved beneath his, and she moaned in her throat as his kiss deepened, his mouth hungry as it plundered the sweetness of hers. Her response was immediate, and they were both overwhelmed by the fierce sweet passion that flared between them.

Alex released her hands, and they crept around his neck, tangling in the darkness of his hair to pull him closer, his body taut and heavy, pressing her into the softness of the bed.

He kissed her throat, his tongue flicking against the pulse that beat so frantically there, then he raised his head.

Their eyes met as Talia pushed the shirt from his powerful tanned shoulders. In the dark silence of the room she could hear the ragged quickening of his breathing, and her own came unevenly. She looked into his grey eyes and her skin heated as though touched by flame. Time didn't exist, nothing existed.

'I want you, Alex,' she whispered, and saw his eyes darken with desperate passion. She let her glance slide to his mouth, warm, beautifully moulded, down to his smooth-skinned shoulders, the broad lines of his chest, matted with fine dark hair, down further to his hard flat stomach.

Then she noticed the scar, and her eyes fixed on it in surprise. It was below his right shoulder, a thick white line of scarred skin, vivid against his tan. His body had been unmarked the last time they made love. Had he been involved in an accident?

She wanted to ask him, but the words didn't come; her mouth was dry, her heart pounding in her ears. His body was beautiful, magnificent, even that jagged white scar added to his aggressive virility. She ran her fingers over it, and that hot desperate ache filled her as she looked at him. His mouth moved against her hair.

'How many other lovers have you had?' he groaned softly.

She looked into his face and saw a rough possessiveness twisting his mouth.

'Is that any of your business?' she asked teasingly, touching his brown throat and wondering at that hard possession.

'No, dammit—I'm sorry.' He suddenly smiled down at her, his expression wry, his eyes still dark with desire. 'Put it down to jealousy.' He kissed her face tenderly.

'There's been nobody else,' she said, telling him because she wanted him to know the truth. 'Nobody.'

Alex closed his eyes for a moment, then his strong arms tightened around her and his mouth parted hers again, flame beating between them as their bodies pressed closer. 'Oh God, Talia. . . .' She could feel the roughness of his chest against her aching breasts, the strong racing of his heart as she kissed him, matching his need with a need of her own.

Their bodies twisted against the cool, smooth sheets in fever, and neither heard the light tapping on the door.

Long seconds passed before the persistent noise finally penetrated Alex's ears. He lifted his mouth from Talia's smooth shoulders, swearing violently under his breath.

The knocking came yet again, louder now. It was fairly obvious that the person knocking was not going to go away.

Alex moved off the bed, pulling on his shirt with angry grace. Talia pulled the bedcovers back up under her chin, her face very flushed as Alex called, 'Come in, Mrs Craven.'

Mrs Craven's grey head appeared round the door, her eyes embarrassed, uncomfortable.

'I'm so sorry, Mr Jordan. . . .' she began worriedly.

'What is it?' Alex looked slightly amused.

'Well, it's. . . .' Mrs Craven looked anxiously at Talia, as though unwilling to say what she had to in front of Alex's new wife. 'Well, it's Miss Dominic on the telephone. I told her that you didn't wish to be disturbed, but she insisted, said it was extremely important that she speak with you. I thought it best to check with you.'

Alex nodded. 'You did the right thing,' he assured her gently. 'I'll take the call in the study.'

He walked over to the door, his eyes dark as he turned and smiled at Talia. She didn't smile back, but closed her eyes, not wanting to see him go. She suddenly felt sick at what she had nearly allowed to happen between them. The raging desire inside her shrivelled into shame, contempt for herself. How could she have let his lovemaking wipe Joanna Dominic from her mind?

As Alex had so bluntly pointed out, this was only a marriage of convenience. It was all for Matty's sake and she felt sure that it would not halt his relationship with his secretary.

The thought of Alex making love to Joanna Dominic, the way he had just made love to her, made her stomach turn over. She was mad, she told herself miserably, mad to have let him touch her again.

She opened her eyes wearily, to find Mrs Craven still hovering uncertainly. 'Are you feeling better, my dear?'

Her voice was genuinely concerned, and Talia managed a weak smile. 'Much better, thank you.'

'I'm glad. Mr Jordan was ever so worried.'

Talia didn't believe that for a moment, and her mouth twisted cynically. 'I drank a little too much champagne,' she admitted ruefully.

'You've got every right on your wedding day, my dear,' Mrs Craven laughed with delight. 'You must be hungry.'

Talia nodded, because it was expected of her, though the thought of food made her feel physically sick.

'Good, good. Dinner is ready any time you are, it's all on the trolley.' Talia smiled again. 'And your little boy is sound asleep. Oh, he's a lovely child, you must be very proud of him.'

'Yes, I am.'

'And Mr Jordan too. I can't tell you how pleased I am for both of you. He's waited a long time for the right young lady, and I knew you were the right one as soon as I saw you,' Mrs Craven rattled on.

What about Joanna Dominic? Talia thought bitterly. She would have been the right one if it hadn't been for Matty, but she remained silent as Mrs Craven bustled from the room, still chattering.

She lay back against the pillows, her eyes suddenly wet with tears. If the housekeeper had not interrupted them, she and Alex would have been making love now. She had wanted him, so badly—a man who cared nothing for her, who had discarded her so carelessly, who had forced her into a loveless marriage. God, how she had wanted him! She buried her face in the scented pillow, her tears turning to sobs that racked her body, her self-respect in ruins.

She did not hear Alex re-entering the room, walking silently to the bedside, only felt the gentle touch of his hand on her shoulder.

'Talia, what is it? Why are you crying?'

She flinched away from him. 'Leave me alone!' Her voice was muffled, her tears coming faster and faster. Alex stared down at her for a moment, his eyes bleak, his wide shoulders strangely tense, then he sat down on the side of the bed, his hands closing on her shoulders, pulling her up and wrapping the sheet around her body, before taking her into his arms.

'No. . . .' She pushed at his chest, but his strength defeated her.

He stroked back her tousled burnished hair. 'Talia, can't we talk?' His voice was weary, almost defeated.

She shook her head mutely. There's nothing to talk about.' She sniffed, trying to control her tears, desperately trying to pull herself together. She did not want to cry in his arms.

'You're unhappy,' Alex said gently.

'I have no reason for being anything else.' She raised tear-washed defiant eyes to his face. 'You forced me to marry you, now you've tried to . . . to seduce me. Why won't you leave me alone? Why are you so cruel?'

'You wanted me,' he reminded her coolly. 'It was a mutual thing. You're only deceiving yourself if you pretend that I was trying to take you against your will——'

'You were angry,' she cut in fiercely, accusing him.

Alex stared at the trembling vulnerable line of her mouth, at the pain in her beautiful eyes and sighed. 'Yes, I was angry,' he conceded wryly. 'You, my sweet Talia, would try the patience of a saint.'

'And we all know that you're no saint,' she said flatly.

He smiled at that, the tension leaving him, and Talia felt her stomach curl alarmingly. It would be so easy to give in, to submit to him. Not only easy but pleasurable. Alex was an expert lover, and he wanted her. But she knew that he would take everything he could, all her secrets, everything precious. It was in his nature to take, to possess. She would be left with nothing. She had offered him everything three years ago and he had flung it all back in her face. She was neither strong or foolish enough to do that a second time.

She pulled herself out of his arms. He let her go easily and she wiped away the last of her tears with her fingers.

'Did you sort out the emergency?' she asked in a cold voice. She didn't want to talk about herself or him. She wanted him to leave the room so that she could shower and dress. She wanted to see Matty. She wanted a cup of coffee and a cigarette.

'Of course.' Alex's voice was cool and unrevealing.

'I don't suppose Miss Dominic was very pleased by our marriage,' she said recklessly, trying to force some sort of reaction out of him.

'Why should you think that?' He stared at her, face expressionless. Talia felt a nameless rage building up inside her. He was such a liar, such a cheat!

'My God, you must think I'm very stupid,' she shot out angrily. 'Do you think you and Joanna Dominic aren't common knowledge?'

Incredibly, Alex began to laugh, his black head thrown back. Talia stared at him, almost speechless with amazement and anger.

'Joanna is my secretary, nothing more,' he said at last, his mouth still curved with amusement.

'Oh, really?' Her voice was acid. He *did* think she was stupid!

'Yes, really.' His smile was infuriating. 'And even if there was something between us, would it really bother you?'

That was the nearest she was going to get to an admission, Talia thought bitterly.

'No, it wouldn't bother me in the slightest, but don't insult my intelligence by imagining I don't know what's going on.'

'You're crazy,' he said softly. 'Absolutely crazy.'

'Not as crazy as you. You should have married her, not me,' she said childishly.

Alex's dark brows rose. 'If I'd wanted to marry her I would have done. I married you, and I'm tired of all these ridiculous games you persist in playing.'

Her colour rose at the boredom in his voice and she felt hurt. 'I'm *not* playing games,' she said in a small voice. 'I hate you, and you can't believe that, can you? Your ego won't accept it.'

Alex's mouth was suddenly hard and cold. 'I don't have to accept it. Ten minutes ago, I could have had you.' His eyes bored relentlessly into hers. 'I could have made you beg me to give you pleasure, to take you. We both know that.' His cold assertions were like salt in her humiliated wounds.

She reached up as fast as lightning and slapped his face with all the force she could muster, her eyes burning with furious hatred for him. Her action seemed to explode something between them. There was a second of unendurable, electric calm, then Alex grabbed her shoulders, his fingers almost snapping her bones, his expression unbearably cynical as he bent his head and began to kiss her savagely. He was punishing her for pushing him too far, and there was no gentleness, no passion in the mouth that roughly possessed hers.

Talia moaned, struggling desperately in his grasp, pushing at his unyielding body in panic. She was shocked by his brutality, threatened by his immense strength, but her body was suddenly yielding, fired by his touch, until finally, as though disgusted with himself and with her, Alex let her go and moved lithely off the bed. Talia saw the cold anger in his eyes, heard the roughness of his breathing as they stared at each other.

That weird, dizzying tension crackled between them and Alex's fists clenched by his sides, the knuckles gleaming bone-white.

Talia opened her mouth to speak, but he was already striding from the room, and the door slammed behind him, the noise echoing in the silence.

CHAPTER EIGHT

THEY ate dinner in strained silence. Talia found her appetite non-existent, even though the food was delicious. The disturbing scene had not affected Alex's appetite, she thought, watching him secretly from under her lashes. He was a dark, remote stranger. It was difficult to remember that such a short time ago he had been holding her in his arms, touching her so passionately. Now it seemed as though he could not even bear to look at her.

'You should eat something,' he suddenly said, his cool voice cutting across her thoughts.

'I . . . I'm not hungry,' she replied dully. His wide shoulders lifted indolently and the silence built up again. Talia sighed miserably. Was this how it was going to be for the rest of their lives? And what did she want, anyway?

They drank coffee and brandy in the lounge. Talia looked round with interest at the rich red walls, at the stone sculptures and the thick pile carpet. It was a beautiful room, stark and unique, yet comfortable, telling of impeccable taste, wealth and masculinity. She glanced at Alex and found him watching her with guarded eyes. She quickly looked away again, wondering how many women he had brought here, how many he had made love to, seduced, in the huge silken bed she had woken in.

Her lips twisted in a bitter half-smile. Seduced? Alex wouldn't have to seduce the women he desired. They would be willing, eager, probably wanting him more than he wanted them.

Her train of thought suddenly halted abruptly, one word flashing in her mind. Jealousy.

She tried to turn away from it, but it wouldn't go, wouldn't be shoved from her mind. It hit her like a bomb blast. She *was* jealous. Jealous of every woman Alex wanted, every woman he made love to, and above all the others, she was jealous of Joanna Dominic.

She lit a cigarette, with shaking hands, and drew on it deeply. She was jealous and it was tearing her apart. It made a mockery of her hatred for Alex, and that worried her. She glanced at him through her lashes. He was still watching her.

'This is a very beautiful flat,' she said with a slight careful smile. It was the first time she had spoken without prompting since before they had sat down to dinner and she felt, rather than saw, his surprise.

He flashed her a brief warm smile. 'Thank you. I chose it primarily for its convenient position.' His voice was deliberately light.

'Do you entertain a lot?' She didn't know why she was asking these questions, something inside was driving her on, even though she knew his answers would hurt her.

'Mm, quite a lot.' His grey eyes were amused, relaxed.

'Women?' she persisted painfully.

He nodded. 'Yes, women.'

'I suppose Miss Dominic is one of your most frequent. . . .' She paused. 'Guests?'

'Joanna has been here a number of times, yes,' he drawled patiently.

'I see.' At least he was being honest.

'I don't think you do.'

'Believe me, I do,' she said bitterly. 'But perhaps in future you could let me know in advance, when you invite her, then I'll know to keep out of the way.'

Alex's eyes flared with irritation. 'I've already told you that Joanna is not my lover. Why do you persist in this? What the hell do you want—a promise of fidelity?'

She felt the heat staining her cheeks. 'No . . . no, of course not. I would like you to be . . . discreet, though—for Matty's sake,' she added hastily. And that was another lie. She did want Alex's fidelity, even though she had no real right to it. She wanted his love, and there was no point in hiding that from herself any longer.

She was in love with him. She had never stopped loving him and she doubted that she ever would. She had been fighting against that realisation ever since she had seen him in the restaurant, but now it had to be faced.

She had tried to hate him, had almost conned herself into believing she had succeeded, but it didn't work that way. She had fallen in love right from the start, a love so deep that even his cruel rejection had not killed it. It was all so hopeless, because he would never love her.

'For Matty's sake?' Alex's mouth was cynical. 'Have you no opinions on the matter, my love?'

'What you do is your own business,' she replied stonily, terrified that now she had admitted to herself that she was in love with him, it would somehow show, that he would look at her and realise.

'How very understanding you are!' Alex's soft drawl mocked her. 'Would you change your mind, I wonder, if you knew that I had no intention of being so tolerant?'

'I don't understand.' She raised clear dark eyes to his, her expression puzzled.

He smiled, though his eyes were hard, serious. 'Think about it,' he suggested mockingly.

She read his expression and almost laughed hysterically. There was absolutely no chance that she would take a lover. He was the only man she wanted, would ever want, but she wasn't going to let him know it.

'I shall do what I please,' she said defiantly, 'and you can't stop me.'

'I wouldn't advise you to put that to the test.' There was a threat behind the cool words. 'I could keep you so occupied, you wouldn't even have time to look at another man.'

His meaning was crystal clear, and she stood up, pushing back her hair, her legs suddenly weak, tired of all the fencing, the arguments. This was not how she had expected to spend her wedding night. She prowled round the room, slender and graceful, restless.

Alex watched her with unfathomable eyes.

'Can't we talk about something else?' she asked tiredly, not looking at him.

'Pulling your head out of the sand at last?' he asked amusedly.

Talia shrugged, not answering.

'Okay,' he conceded, quite gently. 'Let's talk about you and me.'

Talia's head jerked up and she eyed him warily. 'What about you and me?'

'Would you like to fly to Fiji tomorrow?'

'*What?*' Her face mirrored her surprise and her panic.

'It's a perfectly straightforward question.' He lit a thin black cheroot and the fragrant smoke spiralled around the room.

'But why?' she asked stupidly, still not understanding.

'I believe it's called a honeymoon.' His mouth was unbearably mocking.

'No!' Her response was immediate, her face twisting in pain. 'A ... a honeymoon would be ridiculous, given the circumstances of our marriage.'

'Would it?' His eyes darkened as they slid over her silk-clad body, their sensual invitation making her catch her breath.

'You know it would. Anyway, I don't want to go.' Her mind filled with images of white sand and clear green sea, of herself and Alex making love under incredibly blue skies. The images frightened her.

'Are you sure?'

She got the feeling he couldn't care less, one way or the other, and misery engulfed her.

'Sure.' She underlined the one word answer with a cold glare.

'Very well, in that case we'll drive down to the house.'

She knew that he had a house deep in the country, but had never seen it. Alex had told her that they would be living there after they were married. Apparently it was a big house with acres of garden, perfect for Matty.

Talia was pleased, though she didn't tell him so. She wanted Matty to grow up in the country, and the house was near enough to London for Alex to commute and Talia to visit friends and shop. She was looking forward to seeing it.

'Yes, I'd like that,' she answered, and had to stop herself smiling at him.

The telephone began to ring. Alex moved to answer it and she watched his lean graceful body with wonder and a great deal of worry.

She perched herself on the arm of one of the chairs, her mind in turmoil as he talked.

It had been a mistake to think that marrying Alex would be an easy way out of all her problems. Now she knew she was in love with him, she had so many problems she didn't even know where to start. She longed to be reckless, to accept his invitation to go to Fiji. What did it matter, when she wanted him so badly?

If she was sensible, she would take what she wanted, take everything Alex offered, and take it on his terms. She watched him as he talked on the telephone, staring at the hard line of his jaw, his tanned cheekbones, the sensual firmness of his mouth, and the intensity of her love, now admitted without delusion, shook her.

He was a strong, charming, complex man—too complex for her to fully understand, although she had glimpsed many sides to his character. He had a wild reckless streak in his nature, tempered by self-assured strength and a brilliant mind. He could be coldly and utterly ruthless, and yet he had a warm, innate charm and a quality of gentleness that turned Talia's knees to water. He was an enigma, and she ached to know him.

Swinging her legs, feeling utterly confused, she lit another cigarette. It changed everything, of course, this love inside her. It made a lot of things clear.

It was the reason she had given in so easily to his suggestion of marriage. Deep in her subconscious, she had wanted him enough to take a chance and marry him. Had she really hated him, she would have fought like mad against the very idea of becoming his wife. Had she hoped that he would come to love her if they married? It seemed that she was still as stupidly naïve as she had been when she first met him. He would never love her.

And there was still Joanna Dominic. Whatever Alex said, Talia still believed them to be lovers. All the evidence added up that way, and that hurt just as badly as it had done when she first found out. It was a pity she had not thought all this out before the

ceremony, because she still had to face her most
pressing problem. Alex wanted her. She remembered
his hungry grey eyes on her naked body and a fierce
shudder ran through her. How could she fight him
when she desired him so much, when her whole body
melted at his touch? How would she stop him if he
tried to make love to her?

Panic gripped her. She could not bear the pain of
him making love to her when he did not care for her.
She would be just another woman in the long line of
women eager to satisfy his needs.

Alex replaced the receiver and their eyes met. Talia
felt a leaping of her pulses and quickly looked away,
getting to her feet again, anxious for escape.

'I . . . I think I'll go to bed.' Her voice sounded
unnatural, as nervous as a cat.

Alex stared at her for a moment, his eyes
unreadable, then he smiled.

'That sounds like a good idea,' he said softly,
moving towards her, reaching out a tanned hand and
touching her auburn hair.

Talia flinched, jumping back. 'I meant alone.' She
tried to make her voice sound hard, certain, but knew
that it shook alarmingly.

'Do you honestly think I'd let you sleep alone?' he
murmured, staring at her.

She heard the husky invitation in his voice and her
heart began to pound. She could feel her resistance
crumbling as she looked into his brilliant dark eyes.

'You told me you didn't want me,' she remembered
desperately.

'I was lying,' he said with a cool smile. 'My God, I
want you—and you know that.'

Talia swallowed convulsively, desperately trying to
think. The intimacy of their situation made her heart
race. She was alone in this beautiful luxurious flat

with a tall grey-eyed stranger who was her husband. 'Well, I don't want you,' she said breathlessly.

Alex's eyes flared with impatience. 'You're beginning to sound like a cracked record. You're lying to me, you're lying to yourself. You want me.'

'I don't want to sleep with you,' she repeated evenly, staring at the top button of his shirt, at the smooth tanned skin and curling black hair, unable to meet his eyes. 'You lied to me.'

'I saw my chance and I took it,' he replied, watching her relentlessly.

'I might have known that I would have to pay for this lifelong security. Nothing comes for free, isn't that your motto?' Her weakness had turned to anger.

Alex's mouth hardened. 'You knew what I wanted.'

'No, I didn't.' She began to laugh. 'I took you at your word. I only realised today that you expected my body in payment. How stupid can I be?'

He took a step forward, his hand curving round her waist, and she froze, her heart stopping. 'Don't. . . .' she whispered in panic, but he ignored her, his fingers tracing the soft curve of her body beneath the thin silk.

She felt his touch shivering through her, awakening all her nerve endings. She twisted away from him. 'I'll scream,' she threatened in a shaking voice. 'I'll wake Mrs Craven.'

Alex's wide shoulders lifted, his eyes unfathomable. 'Scream,' he said uncaringly. 'I'll put my mouth to yours and you won't make a sound.'

She looked at the power of his body and a strange excitement dried her mouth. Why was she fighting him, anyway? She tried to pull herself together, biting her lip, hating herself for wanting to give in, for that second of weakness. If Alex saw that weakness, he would use it ruthlessly.

'Why should I let you use me?' she demanded, moving across the room. 'I *won't* be used—you don't love me.'

Alex's body tensed. 'And if I did love you?' he asked carefully.

She felt pain tearing at her, that he could talk about love so callously, use the lie for his own ends.

'It wouldn't make any difference, because I don't love you.' She told her lie through clenched teeth.

Alex's mouth twisted. 'You'd like to see me on my knees, though, wouldn't you?'

Her eyes widened at his low words. She did not understand.

'I'm tired,' she said, ignoring the cold question.

'You're a liar,' he bit back. 'You've been asleep all afternoon.' He took a step towards her and she froze. He watched her involuntary action with suddenly blank eyes. Tension threaded between them, tangible, locking them in an explosive awareness of each other. Talia felt dizzy as she looked at Alex's hard mouth.

'Are you deliberately trying to annoy me?' he demanded harshly, and she shrank from the anger vibrating in his voice. 'Because if you are, let me tell you, you're damn well succeeding!'

'Why can't you believe what I tell you?' she almost shouted.

'Because we're not playing games any more, Talia, this is for real.'

'If you need a woman so badly, why don't you ring Joanna Dominic? I'm sure she would be only too happy to accommodate your ... your needs!' she hurled jealously, feeling unbearably hurt, unbearably alive. Every sense in her body was open to Alex. Every time she looked at him, desire ached inside her, and it wasn't easy fighting herself and him at the same time.

He swore harshly, his eyes hard. Talia backed away,

but he was too fast for her. His fingers curled around her slim shoulders, pulling her inexorably forward into his arms, dragging her against the hard strength of his body, one hand tangling in her hair to pull back her head. The mouth that touched hers was ruthlessly angry, the kiss deep, drugging, pushing aside protest, fiercely demanding a response that Talia could not hold back. And when he finally lifted his dark head, she was clinging to his wide shoulders, her body soft and yielding, her dark eyes drowsy as she gazed into the hard lines of his face. He was breathing raggedly and she could feel his heart racing as fast as her own.

'Oh God, Talia, you drive me crazy,' he muttered against her hair, his voice thick with aroused passion. She smiled, her mouth tender, and Alex stared down at her for a moment, then released her.

She stood perfectly still, feeling as though she had been cheated out of something she needed very badly. What was going on?

Alex had his back to her. He was pouring a drink. 'Would you like another brandy?' His voice was harsh, controlled.

'No . . . no . . . thank you.' She stared at the back of his head, her face very hot, her legs weak, trembling.

'You can sleep in the same room—you won't be disturbed.' He did not turn round.

'Yes. Right.' Ridiculously, she felt tears welling up in her eyes. Was he rejecting her? And wasn't that what she had wanted all along? She turned on her heel and practically ran from the room.

Before going to bed, she checked on Matty, feeling miserable and guilty. She hadn't looked after him properly at all today. He was fast asleep, his strong little body curled up, and he was smiling. Talia gazed down at him and began to cry.

When she woke late the next morning after a very

restless night alone in the huge empty bed, her first
thought was Matty. She jumped out of bed and ran to
his room. The bed was empty. She walked into the
lounge, intending to find Matty or Mrs Craven, and
halted at the scene which met her eyes.

Alex sat in one of the huge leather armchairs, with
Matty curled up trustingly on his lap. Alex was
reading a story, Matty looking at the bright pictures.

Talia stared, unnoticed. They were so alike, their
dark heads together. She could see so much of Alex in
Matty.

Alex was laughing, his grey eyes very gentle as he
watched the little boy. Then, as though sensing her
presence, he raised his head and smiled as he saw her
in the doorway. 'We were beginning to think you'd
sleep all day.' His voice was mocking, not unkind, and
his lazy glance slid slowly down over her body, barely
veiled by the thin lace of her nightdress. She felt
herself blushing at that look.

'Mummy!' Matty's face lit up as he saw her. Alex
lowered the child gently off his knee. He ran to her
and Talia scooped him up against her body and
kissed him, his tiny arms flung around her neck in
love.

'Me and man had a story,' he told her, his clear grey
eyes alight with pleasure. 'Me and man had breakfast
too.'

Talia's eyes met Alex's over Matty's head. His
expression was guarded. She watched him stretch his
powerful arms above his head, in a lazy graceful
movement. Her heart began to beat faster.

He looked dark and virile in the bright morning
light, the blue open-necked shirt and tight faded jeans
accentuating the lean tanned strength of his body. She
looked down at Matty and knew that there was
something she had to do, something she had to do

now, before all her courage failed her. She moved closer to Alex.

'Matty,' Her voice was gentle, very serious, and he looked her straight in the eye, his face curious. 'This is your daddy, your very own daddy.'

She heard the hiss of Alex's harshly indrawn breath, but couldn't look at him.

'Man?' Matty's eyes widened innocently, incredulously. For a moment Talia wasn't sure whether or not he understood. She had probably handled it very badly, but she didn't know any other way to do it.

Then suddenly, as he looked down at Alex, his child's face split into an enormous grin of pure delight.

'Daddy,' he said happily.

Talia put him down, caught stock-still by the flaring warmth in Alex's face as he and Matty stared at each other. She had the feeling that somewhere deep inside his mind Matty had already known. He seemed to have instinctively recognised Alex right from the start. She knew at that moment that she had done the right thing, marrying Alex. He and Matty already loved each other; Matty already needed his father.

Talia felt the blockage of tears aching in her throat, the poignancy of the scene in front of her tearing at her heart, as Alex held out his strong arms and Matty rushed into them.

It was more than she could bear. Mingled with the happiness was a sadness, a feeling of loss, and maybe of jealousy, that Matty wouldn't need her so much from now on.

'I ... I'll get dressed,' she mumbled to no one in particular, and fled the room, blinded by her tears.

Back in the bedroom, she flung herself on the bed and sobbed her heart out, her feelings conflicting, confusing her. She seemed to cry for hours, a final release of all the emotion that had been pent up inside her for the past week, until she felt Alex touch her shoulder.

'Talia——' His voice was low and gentle. She buried her face further into the pillows, wishing he would go away. But there was to be no escape, for she felt him lifting her, turning her in his arms. He lifted up her chin with his thumb and stared down at her pale, wet face, his eyes searching hers.

'Don't cry,' he said on a soft groan, and for some reason that made her tears fall faster.

'Oh God, Talia, my love——' There was a torment in his voice. His arms closed around her, he held her tightly, her damp face pressed to his throat. He stroked back her hair with soothing fingers, and his closeness, his strength, somehow comforted her and she finally became still.

Then he wiped her face and smiled down at her, eyes warm yet unreadable.

'I'm sorry,' she sniffed, feeling embarrassed, her heart somersaulting, her hands flat against the broad strength of his chest.

'For what?'

She watched the movements of his mouth as he spoke, the faint white flash of his teeth.

'For crying all over you. Now my eyes are sore.'

Alex touched her face. 'You look beautiful,' he told her huskily.

Her colour rose. 'I'm sure I don't. Where's Matty?'

'Mrs Craven is feeding him milk and biscuits,' he told her with a smile. There was a pause, then he said, 'I want to thank you for what you did just now—it meant a hell of a lot to me, and I know it can't have been easy for you.'

Talia shrugged, flushing even brighter. 'I couldn't let him carry on calling you "man", could I? You're right, it wasn't easy, I was as jealous as anything, but I'm glad it's done. It was worth it to watch the two of you together. He loves you.'

'He's a beautiful kid,' Alex said softly. 'And you're a good mother.' His fingers stroked the delicate bones of her shoulders, sliding beneath the thin lace, their touch burning.

'I wish I could have seen you when you were pregnant.' His voice had changed, become low and strangely rough. They were getting on to dangerous ground and Talia stiffened, her eyes widening with fear.

'I was ugly,' she said flatly.

Alex easily noted her nervous reaction and his fingers stopped moving against her bare skin.

'I can't believe that.' The roughness had gone, the warm charm back on his face.

'It's true.' She tried to smile, but failed miserably. She licked her lips, her body shifting. 'Now, I'd better shower and dress if we're driving down to the house.'

Alex stared down at her for a moment, his eyes narrowed, searching, well aware that she was shutting him out, shying away from any remotely personal conversation, then he released her and stood up.

'We'll leave after lunch,' he told her with a brief hard smile. Talia looked up at him, at his lean powerful body, at his hands resting lightly on his hips and she suddenly felt very lonely.

'Right. After lunch,' she repeated inanely.

'Talia, are you all right?' His voice was gentle and she longed to go into his arms again. He could make everything right. He could protect her from the brutality of the world, he could ease her misery and her loneliness. He could make her laugh, give her more happiness than anybody else. Yet because he did not love her, there might as well have been a great impenetrable wall of solid rock between them, and she was so unsure of herself and her love for him that she did not dare to break down the wall and show herself to him, for fear of being destroyed.

The pain of his first rejection still haunted her and it would have taken more courage than she had ever possessed to open herself up to the possibility of being hurt again. She had trained her body and mind to live safely. It might be lonely and sterile and not very exciting or earth-shattering, but at least it kept her in one piece, it freed her from all the threats of the world, and meant that she could devote all her time to bringing Matty up.

'Yes, I'm fine,' she lied with difficulty.

Alex seemed unsatisfied with her almost-bright answer, about to push the subject, but he only said, 'I think you'll like the house. We should be there in time for dinner. Louise is dying to meet you.'

'Louise?' Talia stared up at him suspiciously. Was Louise some sort of housekeeper? Or even worse, one of Alex's lovers?

He smiled, reading her thoughts. 'What a nasty little mind you have,' he teased softly. 'Louise is a very old friend. I've known her since I was a child. She looked after me—took me in when my mother died.' Talia digested this in silence. She already knew that Alex's father had walked out on him and his mother when Alex was a baby. His mother had died in a road accident when he was twelve. The loss of both his parents so young had made him tough and self-sufficient, obviously moulding his character, explaining, perhaps, his need to have Matty.

'Does she live at the house?' she asked.

'No, but she keeps an eye on it when I'm away. She actually lives in the village, nearby. She was one of my mother's best friends—since their schooldays, I think.

You'll like her,' he said reassuringly, aware that she was a little scared.

'I hope so,' she replied with a smile. Would this woman be a friend? She would have to wait and see.

'Don't worry—it will all work out.' Alex suddenly bent over and brushed her mouth with his.

She stared at him, wide-eyed, opening her mouth to speak, but he had already turned on his heel, and the door closed quietly behind him as he left the room.

As planned, they left after lunch. It was a bright sunny day and the journey was pleasant and relaxed.

Matty, as always seemed to be the case when he got into a car, was bright and talkative, obviously happy. And he was most impressed with Alex's fast black car that ate up the miles with purring ease once they left the congestion of London behind.

And almost before they knew it, the car was turning off the now-narrow country road, through stone-pillared iron gates rioting with purple rhododendron bushes, along a twisting drive until the house came in view.

Talia gasped with pleasure as she saw it, so calm and serene in the afternoon sun, ivy-covered stone, very old, very big and quite beautiful. The car slid to a smooth halt and Alex watched her face as she peered out of the window.

'It's lovely!' She turned to him and smiled with a radiance she had not shown him since their marriage. She heard his breath rasp sharply, the eyes that held hers unsmiling, and wondered if she had said the wrong thing.

Perhaps he imagined she was only interested in his immense riches, she thought wryly.

The enormous front door was opening, and a small slim woman, a white swathe streaking her grey hair, emerged into the sunlight, followed by two Great Dane dogs. Talia recognised her as the woman Alex had been with in the restaurant that first night.

So this was Louise.

CHAPTER NINE

THE following month flew by, and after the initial upheaval of moving into a new house, Talia found her life falling into a pleasant pattern. If it hadn't been for the ache of love inside her, she would have been quite happy.

Louise had proved a friend after all—Matty treated her like a grandmother and in return was spoiled dreadfully. The house itself was lovely—everything she had ever dreamed of. She and Matty spent long afternoons in the sunny gardens, and one evening Alex came home with a tiny black puppy for Matty. It was love at first sight for both of them, and from that day onwards they were never apart.

The bond of love between Alex and Matty grew all the time. Matty idolised his father, chattering about him incessantly, and following Alex around when he was home.

The little boy had bloomed, his skin browned by long days in the sun with Mac—which was what he had named the puppy. He was learning every day and his eyes were bright with a secure contentment. Talia could never remember him being so happy, and that fact alone helped a little whenever she looked at Alex and her heart began to ache. It was what she had always wanted for him, this safe stable home. Alex had been right! He had given Matty everything. And when she looked at her son, Talia could hold no grudge.

For herself, the days were reasonably happy, Alex had bought her a car so that she was not tied to the house. He also employed a woman from the village to clean, leaving her free to devote her time to Matty.

Louise she found a little reserved, but very helpful and friendly and willing to babysit any time. Her husband, Talia discovered, was an incessant traveller, a writer, at present somewhere in Africa, not due back for some months. It was an intriguing marriage. Louise told Talia that she and Johnson were still very much in love, even though they only saw each other for a few months of every year. Their relationship needed space and distance to survive, and Louise seemed perfectly happy to live alone for most of the time, painting in her tiny cottage, with only her dogs and her friends for company. 'Absence certainly makes the heart grow fonder,' she had smiled, as they sat together having tea one afternoon. 'And I suspect that if Johnson and I saw any more of each other, we'd both be driven mad. We'd probably be divorced within a year!'

Talia could understand that in a way Louise needed her own life, her own peace. The months she and Johnson spent together were wonderful honeymoons.

Louise was supremely happy, her love for her husband lay on her like a cloak of calmness, and Talia was envious.

Nothing had improved between herself and Alex. They were polite strangers, never touching each other, never talking with any depth.

Talia's love for him was leaving her strained and restless, constantly on edge whenever they were together, the tenderness he sometimes showed her hurting her more than cruel words. Alex was remote as he watched her nervousness.

The wall between them was getting higher and higher. He would leave early in the morning and often not return until late. He was working very hard, Talia could see it in the tense line of his shoulders, in the tightness of his mouth.

She was still haunted by visions of him with Joanna Dominic. On nights when he did not return until after she was in bed, though never asleep, she tortured herself with thoughts of them together. Had he taken her out to dinner? Taken her home? Had they made love?

One thing was certain—Alex did not desire Talia. He never touched her now, had made no move to touch her since their wedding night. His grey eyes held a blankness whenever he looked at her.

The strain of living like that was taking its toll on both of them. It couldn't go on. There was so much unsaid between them, and Talia didn't dare to approach him for fear of revealing her love.

As the weeks passed, they saw less and less of each other, and she became more and more miserable.

One hot afternoon, when the house was empty and unbearably quiet and she was alone because Matty was at Louise's cottage painting and she didn't have to pick him up until four o'clock, when they would all have tea together, she wandered through the vast comfortable rooms. She restlessly stared at paintings and sculptures, touching polished wood and silk cushions, and wondered where Alex was.

His lean dark face rose in her mind's eye and she bit her lip, a lonely sadness running through her. He filled her every waking moment, she *ached* for him, while he . . . he did not give a damn.

She felt hot, and running up to her room, searched in the tall chest of drawers for a bikini. She would sunbathe for a while, read a book and try to take her mind off him.

She pulled on the tiny black bikini, grimacing at the whiteness of her skin.

The huge empty bed seemed to mock her. Every night she lay in it alone, her body frustrated, filled with energy. She would listen for sounds of Alex, straining her ears in the darkness, longing to go to him, to push aside everything that lay between them.

In the cold light of day, she always resented that weakness, resented Alex's coolness, the fact that none of it seemed to be getting to him.

She turned away, grabbed a blanket and ran downstairs, collecting a book on her way through the lounge. The sun was fiercely hot as she walked through the gardens, burning pleasantly against her bare skin. She wandered quite a way from the house, to the edge of the trees, where the grass was long and cool.

She flung down her blanket and lay down on her stomach, opening the book and staring at the words with determined concentration. The sun beat down on her back, insects buzzed lazily past her ears. The soft air was full of summer noises. However hard she tried to read, her concentration was non-existent, her attention wandering. She felt drowsy, her eyelids heavy, her body relaxed.

What seemed like a long time later—she couldn't tell whether or not she had actually dozed off—she was suddenly wide awake, as she felt a hand stroking slowly down her back.

She jumped, her heart leaping into her throat. She twisted on to her back and found herself staring up into Alex's unsmiling grey eyes.

'Oh!' she gasped, her hand flying to the thundering pulse in her throat. 'You frightened me!'

He smiled, a twisting of his firm mouth. 'You were asleep.'

'Was I?' She felt flustered, lowering her eyes. 'Shouldn't you be at work?' He was too close and in her confusion, her voice sounded sharp, almost accusing.

'Obviously not,' he replied lazily. His smoky eyes moved slowly down her white body, lingering on the swell of her breasts, barely covered by the tiny bikini bra.

Talia felt her skin heating. She wanted to pull the blanket round herself, but to do that would reveal her discomfort, so she lay perfectly still and glared at him.

His eyes finally returned to her face and their glances locked. She stared into his eyes, and her heart began to hammer. She looked away. 'I'm sunbathing,' she said inanely.

'So I see.' His voice was mocking. 'Mind if I join you?'

'I don't suppose I have any choice,' she muttered with ill-grace.

'Got it in one!'

She watched him from beneath her lashes as he moved beside her. He was wearing tight jeans and a black sleeveless vest. His hair was damp, presumably he had just showered.

The sun gleamed on his wide brown shoulders, on the heavy muscles of his arms. Talia swallowed convulsively, moving away. There was nothing to do but lie still and hope he would go away. No such luck! He propped himself up on one elbow and stared down at her.

'Leon telephoned this morning,' he revealed casually.

'How is he?' She smiled as she thought of Leon.

'Fine. Things seem to be working for them.'

'That's good. He loves her so much.' Talia's voice was soft. 'He deserves to be happy.' She glanced at Alex, and her eyes veered away immediately at something in his face.

'Don't we all?' he said expressionlessly.

'Matty is at Louise's. She's teaching him to paint,' Talia said jerkily. He did not reply and a tense silence began to spiral between them.

She racked her brains for something—anything—to say. Why couldn't they act normally? Why was it always so difficult when they were together? He was watching her, she could almost feel the probe of his eyes. Anger flared inside her. He could make it easy, but he didn't even care enough to do that. Perhaps he enjoyed her discomfort.

'You're staring,' she said in a small angry voice.

'Yes.'

She could hear the amusement threading his voice and it angered her further. She hated his coolness, his control, the fact that she had no defence against him. He could crush her so easily, probably without even noticing. She was so vulnerable to him.

'I wish you'd go away,' she retaliated bluntly, putting more distance between them.

'No chance, sweetheart,' he drawled softly, his hand reaching out, his fingers gently stroking her bare leg.

'Don't!' She flinched away, and saw his mouth tightening, his eyes flaring with anger.

'What the hell do you think I'm going to do? Rape you?'

'How should I know?' Her face was flushed and she was hurt by the ice in his voice.

She had seen so little of him over the past month, and now every nerve, every sense was filled with him. He overwhelmed her with his attention. Her mouth began to tremble violently as he leaned over her, tilting up her chin so that he could see her dark eyes.

He searched her face for long seconds. 'Dammit, Talia, I'm sorry.' His slight smile was gentle, coaxing. 'What is it with us, anyway?'

It's that you don't love me, she thought silently, but only shook her head. Alex sighed heavily. Talia looked at his bare shoulders and shivered. She felt lost, exhilarated, angry, very still, so many conflicting emotions, and she had no idea how to cope with them. She lifted her eyes to his, her emotions easily read.

She heard Alex drawing breath unevenly before his mouth touched hers. He kissed her slowly, deeply, possessively, and her response could not be held back, her small hands clenching at his shoulders.

Something seemed to snap inside her. He had not touched her for so long. Her need for him overwhelmed her like a dam bursting.

As their mouths fused endlessly, she sensed his surprise at her passionate response, and wanted to smile.

His mouth left hers then, trailing a path of flame across her cheekbones, chin, throat. Talia arched back her head in submission, every nerve ending aware that his hands were moving on her curved body. His long fingers stroked her heated bare skin, arousing her fiercely. She touched his brown shoulders, his skin was so smooth, muscles tense, touched the black hair that lay against his neck, tangling her fingers in the thick vitality of it. His heart was racing, she could feel it against her body, matching her own beat for beat.

Alex shuddered as she touched him, murmuring her name as he moved so that somehow, she lay beneath him in the long summer grass, the hard strength of his thighs pinning her to the ground.

His hand moved, deftly unclipping the bra of her bikini, exposing her full breasts to his seeking mouth. As his lips gently caressed her skin, she was drowning, knowing only his strength, his expertise, the deep sensual warmth of his lovemaking. How could she deny him when she loved him so much?

She moaned as his lips teased her stiff nipples, arching her body to his mouth.

'Dear God, Talia, you're driving me out of my mind,' he muttered thickly, burying his lean face in the hollow between her breasts. 'I have to have you!' His hands slid possessively over her, and she trembled with a violent urgency that made her dizzy, weak, deaf with the roar of blood in her ears. Her body was lost beneath the demanding pleasure of his touch, but somehow his muttered words of desire pierced her hazy mind, broke the spell that held her so passively in his arms. She began to struggle, almost involuntarily, against his exploring hands, humiliation at what she was allowing him to do finally bringing her back to her senses.

'Alex, no . . .!' She pushed at the hardness of his chest in sudden panic. Her fingers slid against his smooth skin, but he was too strong for her. He kissed her throat, the warm hungry touch of his mouth sending tremors of excitement through her. She looked down at him through half-closed eyes, her mouth dry, her naked body shivering, aching with a desire that only he could assuage.

It was what she wanted more than anything in the world. She wanted him so much, she couldn't think straight. It would be so good, so pleasurable to let him take her, yet if they became lovers again he would know how she loved him, and it would still mean nothing to him. She would be laying herself open to pain and humiliation.

She swallowed painfully. Fear tore through her at the thought of going through that again. How could she stop him? What could she do? She felt his mouth against her shoulder. 'Another payment?' she asked, in a cold shaking voice, cringing as the words reached her ears. 'Is that what this is, Alex?

Collecting on the security you've given Matty and me?'

For a moment she thought he had not heard her. An awful explosive silence rang in her ears, then he stiffened, his whole body tensing against hers. He lifted his head and stared at her with hard blank eyes, his mouth very angry.

'Damn you, Talia—if that's how you want to see it, then yes, it is!' His face was taut, immobile as it swooped, his mouth savagely parting hers, the burning heat of it shocking her into stillness. He was violently angry, almost beyond control. She felt his hands sliding up her body, closing over the thrust of her breasts, his fingers still gentle, stroking delicately.

He hates me, she thought hysterically, and he hates himself for wanting me. The desire aching inside her, so desperate for release, shrivelled, and she suddenly felt very, very cold. She lay staring up at the intensely blue sky with blind eyes, feeling his mouth, his hands on her. Unnoticed, silent tears fell from her eyes, soaking her face. His touch was tearing her apart, she was hurting so much she thought she might die. What had she done? Why had she provoked this bitter anger?

She heard Alex swearing viciously. He was moving, abruptly sitting up away from her. She couldn't move. She just lay there, staring at his back, watching him rake a quick impatient hand through the blackness of his hair.

Then she realised that she was crying as her breath caught on a noisy sob. She shivered, listening to Alex's uneven breathing. He was very tense, very angry. It was her own fault. She had unleased this dark violence in him. But there had been no other choice for her. She felt as though her body was made of stone.

'For God's sake, don't cry,' Alex grated suddenly, not turning.

'I ... I'm sorry.' She didn't know why she was apologising. She felt almost frightened of him. He swore again at her whispered words, then turned to look at her, his blank eyes sliding over her, taking in the tousled hair, falling around her pale damp face, the soft white curves of her half-naked body.

For a second she just stared into his hard forceful face, then she sat up, fumbling with the bra of her bikini, fingers trembling as though with fever.

Alex watched her impassively. She could read no expression at all in his face, but waves of tension emanated from him, winding round them both.

Talia folded her arms across her breasts, instinctive protection, and sat in silence, head lowered, very flushed. She didn't know what to say to him. She felt awful.

Alex stared at her broodingly, then his hand reached out to push her hair from her face, his thumb gently wiping away a last salty tear.

She flinched at his touch, still afraid of him, of herself, and his hand dropped quickly.

'Don't worry,' he drawled coldly. 'I have no intention of jumping on you—you're quite safe.'

'I didn't think——'

'No? Come off it, Talia, you're as transparent as glass.' His mouth twisted in a smile that did not reach the steel of his eyes.

Did he already know that she was in love with him? She turned away from the thought in horror. 'How clever you are, then,' she marvelled acidly.

Alex laughed. 'You think so?' His voice was cold and hard and mocking.

'Go to hell!' she retorted, turning away, her nerves raw.

He was completely in control of himself. Looking at him, it might have been a different man who, only minutes ago, had been making love to her so urgently. Now he was remote, as cold as ice, totally uncaring.

'Tomorrow I fly to Honolulu,' he told her expressionlessly, as though she had not spoken. 'And when my business there is concluded, I shall move back into the flat in London. You and Matty will continue living here. I'll want to see him, of course— we'll arrange the details when I get back. Don't worry, you'll both be well looked after.'

Talia stared at him open-mouthed. She couldn't have been more shocked if he had hit her. He was leaving. It's what you want, she told herself, and knew it was a lie. She loved Alex deeply, he was a part of her, woven into her heart, her soul. He had brought her back to life after three years of emptiness. The thought of losing him was unbearable.

'But ... but this is your house,' she protested inanely, fighting herself, desperately trying to pluck up the courage to beg him to stay.

'And you're my wife,' he told her with grim unconcern. 'But what the hell difference does it make? Maybe you were right—it was a mistake to force you to marry me. I was wrong, I thought——' He broke off, shrugging his wide shoulders as though the whole subject bored him.

'Alex, please. . . .' She almost reached out to grab his arm, she felt so sick, so cold, only fear that he would reject her holding her back. She couldn't get over that fear.

'There's nothing more to say,' Alex said dismissively, moving to his feet in one lithe graceful movement.

'Don't I have any rights at all to an opinion on this?' Talia demanded unsteadily. She couldn't let him walk away, she just couldn't.

'You've made your opinions crystal clear.' He

glanced down at her through narrowed, unfathomable eyes, his voice curt. 'Goddammit, Talia, you've won—your coldness defeats me, I have no desire to live with a woman who so obviously hates my guts. I think we both know that whatever we had—if we ever had anything—is over. It's better that we live apart.'

'But we could try——'

He didn't give her time to finish. 'It was my mistake. I don't want to see you suffering for the rest of your life for that. Do you think it gives me any pleasure to see you flinching every time I touch you? Do you think it isn't obvious that you're tense and nervous every time we're in the same room? Let's face it—it's over.'

The words were bitten out with furious defeat, and before she had a chance to reply he was striding back towards the house, leaving her staring after him, still shocked to the core by his sudden decision.

Five minutes later she heard the low roar of the car as it shot down the drive. He had gone.

How she got through the rest of the day she had no idea. Time passed in a haze, and although she talked and acted almost normally, it was all mechanical. She had put herself on automatic, while her mind thought and thought and *thought* about Alex. Then at last she was alone in her room, the day's tasks over, Matty asleep. She sank down on to the softness of the bed in utter desolation. She looked at the clock. It was after midnight. Alex would not come back now.

She was all on her own from now on and it was a bleak prospect. She loved him so deeply, living without him seemed impossible. He had never wanted her, though, it had always been Matty.

They should have talked. If only she had shown him some warmth, perhaps he would have come to care for her. At that moment, she would have taken him on any terms at all. She had been cold and bitter, so fearful of being hurt again. She almost smiled. Hurt? Wasn't she hurting now? Wasn't it agony to know that she wouldn't see him again?

They would be polite strangers whenever he came for Matty. How would she be able to bear that? What was the satisfaction worth of knowing that Alex hadn't guessed how she felt? It was worth nothing when she looked at the future in front of her, stretching ahead like a barren desert. And when she looked back, the best times of her life had been spent with Alex, even though they had been the most difficult. Without him she felt barely alive, and her pride was ugly, worthless and destructive.

At eighteen she had given herself fully in love and innocence. The trauma of Alex's rejection had locked her in ice. She had been so determined that he would never hurt her again, determined he would never know how she loved him, determined to fight him every inch of the way.

As he said, she had won, but she had only succeeded in ruining her own life. How could she have been so stupidly illogical? She sighed, turning her face into the cool pillow

Perhaps in the back of her mind she had wanted revenge. Alex had not hidden his desire for her. Perhaps she had denied him out of spite, hoping to hurt him as he had hurt her.

He would find comfort elsewhere. Joanna Dominic would be more than happy to oblige—any woman would. Alex had a magnetic attraction that few women could resist. Including myself, Talia thought ruefully. She rolled off the bed, exhausted, yet so restless. She lit a cigarette and silently paced the room, the thin silk of her nightdress rustling around her tense body. Her mind was running in circles and her head ached.

There was nothing she could do. It was too late. Even if she went to him, begged him to stay, told him that she loved him, it would make no difference. Nothing could change the fact that he did not love her: he had made that very plain. She felt tears welling up in her eyes again. Oh God, she thought desperately, why can't he care?

Images of him with Joanna Dominic, her black hair thrown against his shoulder, tormented her with cruel piercing clarity, until she cried out with the pain of it.

On impulse, she picked up the telephone beside her bed and dialled the number of the flat in Knightsbridge. There was no answer. He must be with her. He must be!

'Damn you, Alex,' she whispered painfully.

He had cracked the ice, cracked it wide without even trying. She felt raw and hurt, unable to cope without him.

She lay down on the bed again, staring at the ceiling, and lit another cigarette. Her hands were trembling. There would be no second chance.

Somehow, as the pink dawn filtered through the lace curtains, she slept. Her dreams were haunted, dark and frightening, and when she woke very late the next morning, she found Matty bouncing on the end of her bed, grinning at her.

He was dressed, she realised, as she struggled into a sitting position, pushing her burnished hair out of her face. She held out her arms and he flung himself into them.

'Daddy was here!' he exclaimed joyfully, against her throat. 'He dressed me.'

Talia's heart leapt. 'Where is he?' she asked, staring down at Matty's black head.

'He's gone,' the little boy told her happily. 'We

come to see you, but you were asleep. Daddy said we can't wake you.'

'Gone?' She felt suddenly sick. He had not even wanted to talk to her. He and Matty had watched her sleeping, then he had gone, without a word. Her heart contracted in fearful pain.

'Yes.' Matty hugged her tightly, his tiny strong arms wrapped around her neck. 'Daddy said I got to look after you.' He smiled angelically. 'Get up now.'

Before she could answer, there was a light tapping on the door and Louise appeared, carrying a tray. 'I've brought your breakfast, my dear,' she said with a smile, and when she saw Talia's surprise, explained, 'Alex telephoned me and I offered to come over and keep an eye on Matty.'

She set down the tray at the bedside and pulled open the curtains, letting the morning sunshine stream in. 'It's a glorious day.'

'Alex telephoned you?' Talia repeated, aghast, her sleepy mind spinning, unable to take everything in.

'Yes, he said you were tired—and I must say, my dear, you do look a little peaky. Perhaps you should stay in bed this morning,' Louise fussed elegantly.

'No . . . no really, I'm fine,' Talia said distractedly.

'You know best, of course.' Louise smiled again and held out her hand to Matty. 'Come on, young man, let's leave your mother in peace to eat her breakfast.'

Matty clambered obediently off the bed and they disappeared, the door closing quietly behind them.

Talia looked at the breakfast tray, uncovered a plate of eggs and bacon and quickly covered it again; the mere sight of it made her feel sick.

She couldn't eat a thing. She poured herself some strong coffee and lay back against the high mound of pillows. Alex had come back after all. She thought of him watching her as she slept and her face burned with embarrassed colour. She sipped her coffee.

Matty seemed very happy this morning; what had Alex said to him? she wondered. Obviously Louise knew nothing, she thought it was just another business trip. Why hadn't Alex explained the situation to Louise? Everything seemed unfinished, up in the air. Why, oh, why hadn't he waited?

Half an hour later she dragged herself from the soft comfort of the bed, showered and dressed. She felt tired, lethargic and very unsure of herself. She couldn't get Alex out of her mind for a single second, her need for him was aching inside her like a terrible pain that nothing could cure.

She paused as she reached the bottom of the stairs. For Matty's sake, she had to appear normal, as though nothing had happened. He was a sensitive, intelligent child, easily affected by her moods and she couldn't bear to upset him.

She took a deep steadying breath, her mind spinning back three years. The same feelings were burning inside her now. She had coped with it once, even though she had thought she would never recover. She only hoped and prayed she could do it again.

CHAPTER TEN

Two days later Leon called. Talia was curled up in an armchair reading, her eyes following the words, while her mind was far away.

She heard the front door bell and sighed, resenting the intrusion. She was enjoying the fragile peace of a morning alone. She got up and slowly trudged to the front door.

'Leon!' Her smile was genuine. She stared into his rugged face and realised how glad she was to see him.

'Hello.' He bent and kissed her cheek.

'Come in.' She shut the door and led him into the lounge. 'Can I get you a drink, or a cup of coffee? I've just made some.'

'Coffee would be fine.' Leon watched as she poured the coffee.

'It's lovely to see you,' she said, meaning it, and sat down opposite him, her knees tucked under her chin.

'I was passing—visiting an old colleague who lives on the coast. Actually I wanted to invite you and Alex out for lunch.'

Talia bit her lip. 'Alex is away on business.' She could almost see what Leon was thinking. 'Honolulu,' she added inconsequentially.

Leon nodded, his blue eyes probing. 'I see—and Matty?'

'Oh, he's with Louise—she's an old friend of Alex's family. They get on incredibly well, they spend hours painting together——' She stopped, aware that her tongue was running away with her. It was such a relief to get off the subject of Alex.

'How are you, anyway?' she asked brightly. 'How are the children and Alicia?'

Leon smiled. 'Alicia and I are doing just fine—we've had our ups and downs, as you can imagine, but I know it's going to work this time.' He lit a cigar, the fragrant smoke drifting on the bright air. 'Belle and Vinnie are back at school and I think Jake is finally getting over you—he's started taking out a girl from one of the local farms. You and Alex must come to dinner—the children would love to see you.'

'I'd like that,' she said, carefully noncommittal. She felt sure Alicia wouldn't be too keen on that idea.

'I'll call you and arrange it. When are you expecting Alex back?' he asked casually.

'I . . . I'm not exactly sure . . . I. . . .' To her utter horror, she suddenly burst into tears, her hands coming up to cover her face. 'Oh dear, I'm so—sorry.' She sniffed, feeling foolish.

Leon produced a clean handkerchief, and handed it to her. 'Here, use this.' His voice was low and kind and made her cry even more.

A moment later she felt his arms go round her and she was held tightly against his chest. The closeness comforted her, and at last she quietened, blowing her nose and looking at him uncertainly.

Leon rose to his feet, looked round the room and smiled. 'I think you could use a drink,' he said firmly, and poured her a large brandy, pressing the glass into her hand.

Talia sipped it gratefully, feeling its warmth seeping into her chilled bones. 'Thank you,' she whispered, her dark eyes apologising.

'Tell me all about it,' he suggested calmly.

'There's nothing——'

'Talia, I could tell that something was wrong the moment I arrived. You look as though you haven't been sleeping, you're tense and worried, yet you're trying to tell me that everything's fine?' he teased, though his eyes were serious. 'Come on, tell me. Maybe I can help.'

She was silent for a moment, then suddenly she blurted out, 'Our marriage is over, Leon—over!' Her voice broke on the last word.

It was such a relief to be able to talk honestly about it. Her nerves were at breaking point with the effort of maintaining a happy façade in front of Matty and Louise.

'What do you mean, over?' His voice was still calm, but she could tell that he was surprised.

'Alex won't be coming back,' she revealed flatly. 'And—oh, Leon, I don't think I can bear it!'

'What happened?'

'I should never have agreed to marry him,' she trembled miserably. 'It's been a disaster right from the start. I thought I could handle the situation, but I. . . .'

'You're in love with him?' Leon hazarded shrewdly.

Talia smiled bitterly. 'Is it that obvious?'

'You wouldn't be so miserable if you didn't care.'

'I wish to God I didn't. How do you stop loving somebody who doesn't give a damn about you? How?' she demanded desperately. 'I can't get Alex out of my mind for a single second!'

'Are you sure he doesn't love you?' There was a strange tone to his voice, but perhaps it was only surprise.

'Absolutely sure. He's never loved me. Even at the beginning, I meant nothing to him.' She could feel the tears blocking her throat again, hot stupid tears of self-pity and sadness.

'Talia, don't upset yourself.' Leon's eyes were dark with concern.

'Upset myself?' she laughed hysterically. 'I *want* to upset myself. I've had to pretend that everything is just fine over the past two days, and the strain is killing me.' She stared at Leon with wide hurt eyes. 'I tried so hard to hate him, but I couldn't. Even when I got that damned telex from South America—even then I still loved him, can you believe that? Now he's gone for good and I don't know what to do.'

'Hey, slow down,' Leon said quietly. 'Let me catch up. Telex? South America?'

Talia lifted her hands impatiently. 'It was before Matty was born. There was some kind of revolution over there and Alex's friend was killed. He had to go over and sort everything out.'

'Yes, I remember,' Leon said thoughtfully. 'Chris Pendal—it was a tragedy. But I still don't understand.'

Talia sighed. 'I'd been seeing a lot of Alex before he went. He promised to keep in touch, but I didn't hear a thing until his secretary gave me a telex he'd sent. Is there such a thing as a "dear John" telex?' Her mouth drooped. 'He didn't even bother to tell me himself— that hurt more than anything else.'

Leon was frowning, his dark brows a straight heavy line. 'Are you saying Alex sent you a telex from South America?' he asked in slow disbelief.

Talia stared at him uncomprehendingly. 'Yes, that's exactly what happened. It was the worst thing——'

'Talia, you must have it wrong. It's an impossibility.'

Her dark eyes searched his. 'What does it matter, anyway? Whatever the finer details, I got a telex from Alex telling me to get lost. That is a matter of fact.'

'Is it?' Leon smiled grimly. 'Did you get it through the post? Was it sent on?'

'No, actually, it was given to me by——'

'Don't tell me, let me guess,' Leon cut in sardonically. 'The efficient Miss Dominic?'

'Well, yes,' Talia admitted slowly, thinking he had gone mad. 'But, Leon, I still don't understand what you're getting at. Why pick on the telex? It's of no importance.'

'It finished you and Alex once and for all, didn't it?'

The pain glittered in her eyes. 'Yes, of course it did.'

'Well, let me tell you something. At the time I had a number of business interests over there myself. I talked to Alex on the telephone, the day before he flew out, because there was a chance that I might have had to go over there. Neither of us were sure of the situation and he promised to try and contact me as soon as he'd got in touch with my main man. I heard nothing from him after that. I learned later that the rebels had seized all lines of communication—nothing was going in or out, even the media had no idea what was going on. The republic was completely sealed off. There were rumours flying round the city that Alex was dead—shares were up one minute and down the next. Do you understand what I'm telling you? There was no way Alex could have got a message—let alone a telex—out. No way,' he emphasised strongly.

Talia stared at him blankly. What was he saying?

'But I . . . I received the telex,' she said stupidly. 'I wrote him a letter when I hadn't heard anything in over a month. I gave it to. . . .'

'Joanna Dominic.' Leon's mouth was angry.

Talia nodded. 'She said she'd send it with some papers——'

'She wasn't sending anything—nobody was. Alex disappeared as soon as he set foot on South American soil. There wasn't a word from him in four months, the company was in panic.'

Talia lit a cigarette with hands that trembled violently and slowly let Leon's words sink in. Joanna Dominic had not forwarded her letter, and the telex. . . .

'Are you *sure* the telex couldn't have come from Alex?' she asked in a small shocked voice.

'One hundred per cent sure,' Leon said firmly. 'Alex was shot four weeks after he arrived. He spent three months in a military hospital—he almost died. Even if the opportunity had been there, which it wasn't, he was in no damned condition to be sending telexes. You've got to believe that.'

'*Shot?*' Talia's stomach turned over in panic. 'Oh, God—shot?'

'I don't know any details, except that he was flown back to England and was in hospital for months afterwards. He was out of commission for almost a year. Surely you knew about it?' Leon was very surprised.

'No, I didn't. After the telex, I thought. . . .' She ran a distracted hand through her hair, her mind bursting. 'If he didn't send it. . . .'

'Joanna Dominic dreamed it up,' Leon grimly finished the equation.

'But . . . but why? For all she knew, I might have been aware that communications were down.'

'She's a desperate woman. I guess it was a calculated risk, and it paid off. You believed her.'

Talia was horrified, deeply shocked. 'How could she . . . how could anybody do a thing like that?' she whispered, appalled at such deliberate destruction.

Leon moved, took her hand. 'I guess she wanted Alex,' he said simply. 'Wanted him so badly she was prepared to go to any lengths to get him. She must have guessed that he was involved with you, especially after you gave her the letter. A vulnerable eighteen-year-old—you were easy game for a calculating bitch like her.'

Talia's face was deathly white. 'I can hardly believe it.' she said in a strained voice. 'It's the most awful thing I've ever heard!'

'At least now you know the truth,' Leon said gently.

She looked at him, caught by something in his voice. She saw how angry he was.

He smiled wryly as their eyes met. 'I could strangle her myself!'

Talia smiled weakly, still shivering with reaction and shock. 'I'll supply the rope!' She touched Leon's arm. 'Thanks for telling me.' She was making a big effort to pull herself together. She would sift through all she now knew, when she was alone.

'It's incredible that you didn't already know,' he told her.

She sighed. 'Circumstances were against me—the telex, the fact that I was pregnant and sure that Alex didn't want anything to do with me. I was in an inpenetrable daze of misery for nine months. I don't suppose I would have noticed if the sky had fallen in.'

'Star-crossed lovers?' Leon suggested with a smile.

'Hardly. It doesn't mean that Alex loves me.'

It didn't change the fact that although he hadn't sent the telex, he hadn't bothered to contact her on his return to England. He hadn't even rung. All Leon had revealed was that Alex had not sent the telex that had broken her heart.

'It does mean you don't know everything. You thought you had it all worked out, now you know you didn't. It must prove something, mm?' Leon said drily, his meaning clear, his smile encouraging.

Talia smiled back, her eyes bright with tears. 'You're wonderful,' she said huskily, and kissed his cheek. 'You've made my day.'

'And you're only the first on my list,' he laughed, and hugged her tightly.

She refused his offer of lunch. He understood that she was in no mood for food. When he had gone she sank back into her chair, still amazed by his revelations. She had lived for so long with the idea that Alex had sent that damned telex, it was difficult to accept that he hadn't.

She could remember so vividly how she had felt on reading it, how everything had crumbled around her. It had been an integral part of her life for three years, it had been her only reality.

She began to laugh, tears rolling down her face. *Alex hadn't sent the telex.*

She thought of Joanna Dominic, wanting to feel sorry for her, but angrily hating her. Was she with Alex now, in Honolulu? It was more than likely, and more than Talia could bear. She buried her face in her hands, shaking uncontrollably.

That afternoon, she sought out Louise, whom she found sketching in the garden. The older woman watched Talia approaching, with a smile.

'I've made some tea,' Talia said brightly, her voice artificial to her own ears.

'Lovely!' Louise tossed her sketchbook on to the table.

Talia poured, glancing at Louise now and again from under her lashes. Louise had known Alex for years and years, she would know all about that time in South America. Talia had so many unanswered questions, her head was bursting with them.

She poured the tea, then settled back, enjoying the sun on her face, and wondering where to start. She felt a little nervous of Louise. The older woman was always so calm and elegant, she always made Talia feel like a scruffy child. She glanced at Louise's beautifully-cut trousers and casually chic blouse, then at her own faded jeans and tight tee-shirt, and sighed. She and Louise were a million miles apart.

'What is it, my dear?' Louise had heard that defeated sigh.

Talia shrugged. 'Nothing,' she replied automatically. Then, 'No, that's a lie. I wanted to ask you about Alex.' She said it quickly, before her courage failed her.

'Ask away.' Louise's wise eyes fixed on her flushed face.

Talia took a deep breath, hardly knowing where to begin. 'I wanted to ask you about South America. He was injured, shot. . . .' She felt her mouth trembling. Pain clenched inside her whenever she thought of him being shot, hurt, whenever she thought of that jagged scar on his powerful brown body.

'Yes, he was shot. What did you want to know?'

Talia had the impression that Louise was angry about something.

'Everything,' she said simply.

'But surely——' Louise broke off abruptly and reached for the silver case on the table, extracting one of the small cigars she smoked and lighting it before continuing. 'You'll have to forgive me, Talia, I'm being unforgivably rude. I'm afraid I'm turning into an interfering old woman.' She lifted her hand as Talia opened her mouth to protest. 'I'm very fond of Alex, and it's been difficult not to notice that there's something wrong between the two of you.'

Talia flushed, lowering her head in silence.

'You were quite a surprise, you know,' Louise continued, with a smile. 'When Alex told me he was marrying you, I must confess I had my doubts. He's always had that romantic streak in him, even as a child.' Her voice was filled with affection.

Talia stared. 'Doubts? But I'd never met you.' Had Louise got her mixed up with somebody else?

'Nevertheless, I knew a lot about you, and I'm afraid when Alex brought you here, I wasn't sure if we could be friends.'

'I don't understand—please explain,' Talia cried in confusion. She felt as though she was going mad. 'Has Alex said anything about . . .?'

'Alex has never discussed you—he wouldn't.' Louise sighed, tapping the ash from her thin cigar. 'I really have no right to interfere. It's between Alex and yourself.'

'But why didn't you like me?' Talia persisted. Something inside her was telling her that Louise had the key to all this confusion, and she *had* to know.

'Quite simply because when Alex was so ill, calling out for you night and day, you refused to see him,' Louise said quietly, obviously discomfited.

'I did *what*?' Talia's mouth dropped open in astonishment. 'Louise, you *have* to believe me, I only found out this morning that Alex had been shot while he was in South America.' She closed her eyes. 'I think I'm going mad!'

Louise patted her arm. 'I'm sorry, my dear, I shouldn't have said anything.'

'Tell me,' Talia begged, her eyes enormous in her pale face. 'Tell me everything, please, it's so important!'

Louise stared at her for a moment, then sensing her urgency, lifted her hands in a gesture of acquiescence. 'Apparently Alex was caught in some crossfire between the rebels and the government forces. He was on his way from the hotel to the company building. He was taken to a military hospital—the condition there must have been appalling, because by the time he was flown home, the wound was infected, he had a fever and there was a chance of blood poisoning, of him losing his arm.' She paused, obviously upset by the memories. 'I spent weeks at the hospital. He asked for you over and over again. Of course I had no idea who you were or where I could find you, but Talia is such an unusual name. I asked Miss Dominic, who was also visiting regularly. She knew you she promised to contact you and ask you to come to the hospital. You never came, and so I thought. . . .'

'Oh God!' Talia found herself shaking again, tears pouring down her face. 'I didn't know,' she said desperately. 'I didn't know!'

'Miss Dominic didn't contact you?'

'Never. I swear to you, she didn't. I thought . . . I thought Alex didn't want to see me. I would have come. . . .' She couldn't speak any more.

Louise watched her with distressed eyes, before putting her arms around the younger girl and comforting her, the first real bonds of friendship growing in that moment.

Finally Talia quietened, wiping her face, her eyes red and desolate. She felt weak with the horror, the trauma of it all.

Louise smiled and poured out more tea for them both, giving Talia time to compose herself.

Talia lit a cigarette and drew on it deeply, forcing herself to feel calm. She thought again about the scar on Alex's body. He had asked for her. He *had* cared. That meant everything, even though it was too late. She looked at Louise through dull eyes. 'I had no idea,' she repeated huskily. 'I didn't even know that Alex had been shot.'

'Miss Dominic has a lot to answer for,' Louise said coldly. 'If I'd have even suspected. . . .'

'It's too late now.' Talia stirred her tea, gazing into the pale liquid, her shock at Joanna Dominic's deceit numbing her. 'It's all in the past. Alex won't be coming back.'

'You're in love with him,' Louise said gently.

'Yes, but everything is ruined. You see, I thought Alex had rejected me. Ever since we got married— well, there's no point in dragging it all up. It's over.'

'There's Matty,' Louise reminded her. 'Alex loves him dearly.'

Talia nodded silently. She felt very cold, very raw. 'But he doesn't love me.'

'Are you sure of that?' Louise was suddenly smiling. 'Knowing Alex as I do, I'd say that you were wrong. Oh, I know he's a very private man, but when he was lying in that hospital, his defences were down and there was no doubt that he loved you very deeply. When you didn't come, he closed himself away, he became hard and bitter and hell to live with.' She smiled slightly, remembering. 'I thought that was all over since you married, but perhaps he's afraid to reach out for you again, afraid to lay down his pride and open his heart to you. As afraid as you are to do the same.'

Talia listened carefully to the wise words, trying to squash the tiny flaring of hope in her heart. Had Alex loved her? Was there *any* chance that he still cared after all that had happened between them? Her life was worth nothing without him. She had to take a chance.

'Miss Dominic. . . .' she began uncertainly, still haunted with doubt.

'Alex married you,' Louise said firmly. 'Oh, I know, she was there during the worst time of his life. She was offering more than comfort. Alex may have taken her out a few times, but he never cared for her—I'd stake my life on that.'

Talia listened. She *had* to take a chance. 'What shall I do?' she asked tremulously, eagerly.

Louise raised her fine eyebrows. 'I think you already know. Now, don't worry about a thing, I'll look after Matty while you're away.'

'I don't know where Alex is,' said Talia, panic gripping her. Everything was moving so fast.

'I have the address,' Louise smiled, and pulled a folded piece of paper out of her pocket.

Talia looked at it and laughed. 'Did you know?'

Louise only smiled. 'You'd better book your flight.' She saw the uncertainty in Talia's eyes and added, 'You love him, my dear. Don't let him slip through your fingers. Don't let Miss Dominic stand in the way of your happiness.'

Talia jumped to her feet, her face radiant, beautiful. 'Thank you for being so wise!' She kissed Louise's cheek and ran towards the house.

CHAPTER ELEVEN

SHE could only get a flight via Los Angeles, and it seemed to take days and days to get to Honolulu.

She hired a car and bought a map as soon as she got there, then checked into a large hotel on Waikiki beach, showered and changed her clothes.

Nerves were fluttering madly in her stomach as she forced herself to sit on the balcony of her room and sip a long iced drink.

Below her stretched miles of pale sand, dotted with palm trees, crowded with sunbathers, and the startlingly blue-green ocean, the whole view dominated by the towering Diamond Head Volcano. It was beautiful, a paradise, a holidaymaker's dream.

The trouble was that Talia was no holidaymaker. She was here to try and save her marriage to a man she loved so deeply she could not bear to think of failure.

She sipped her drink, blindly staring out across the dazzling ocean. She was here at last. She had not allowed herself to think too deeply about what she was doing. Had she allowed herself that luxury, she felt sure her courage would have failed her. It seemed years since she had been sitting on the lawn with Louise—yet it had only been yesterday.

She pushed the heavy weight of her hair away from her face, wiping the fine beads of perspiration from her forehead, shading her eyes from the relentless sun. She was filled with doubts. What would she say to him? How could she explain?

She had no real idea whether he still cared. She was taking the biggest gamble of her life, opening herself wide to the agony of his rejection. But when she thought of the alternative, a life without him, she knew that she had to do it. She bit her lip savagely and got to her feet.

She would go to the beach house now, while she still had the nerve. She walked through the room, grabbing her handbag, then glanced at herself in the long mirror.

A tall slim girl stared back at her, thick shining hair falling around her shoulders, huge dark eyes in a tense, unsmiling face. The brief shorts she was wearing accentuated the long smoothness of her legs, the short-sleeved blouse brought out the colour of her hair. She wanted to be beautiful. 'But beggars can't be choosers,' she said to herself, still wondering if she should change into something more respectable.

She was playing for time, she realised, and hastily left the room.

She easily found the beach house Alex was staying at while concluding his business in Honolulu. It was enormous, obviously owned by someone extremely wealthy. She was actually trembling, her palms damp as she pulled the car off the road and down the long palm-lined drive. It was madness to come here—madness. But too late to turn back.

The car slid to a halt. Talia climbed out, took a deep breath, walked to the door, rang the bell and waited. There was no answer. She rang again. Please let him be here, she prayed, her heart beating loud and fast. Still no answer.

Dry-mouthed and rigid with nerves, she walked round the side of the low house, wondering if there was some back door she could try. If not, she would have to wait until he returned. She would never have enough courage to do this a second time.

She turned the corner and stopped dead in her

tracks. Down on the pale beach in front of her, Alex stood alone at the water's edge. He was staring out towards the horizon, smoking idly. Talia stood perfectly still and watched him. He was wearing old jeans, tight around his lean hips, and a sleeveless blue vest, his powerful shoulders gleaming and tense. She was struck by his aloneness. I love him, she thought fiercely, and walked slowly towards him, her sandalled feet silent in the hot powdery sand.

But as though some sixth sense warned him of her approach, he turned when she was only feet away from him, his grey eyes narrowing, his expression guarded.

'Hello, Talia.' He greeted her coolly, not smiling, not surprised. She thought her legs were going to give way under her and her heartbeat was deafening her.

'Why have you come?' His eyes slid over her, lingering on the long length of her legs, the pulse flickering in her throat.

'I . . . I. . . .' She looked away. What could she say? I love you? Glancing at him, she could not believe he had ever cared for her. He was so cold and remote, a powerful, alien stranger. She bit her lip, the sunlight burning in her hair.

Alex watched her, his face unreadable. The tense silence lengthened.

'Alex, I. . . .' The words wouldn't come. 'I don't know what to say to you,' she whispered.

'Do you want a drink?' His voice was expressionless. She nodded in silence, and walked beside him through sliding glass doors, hung with bamboo blinds, into a large lounge, with a cool marble floor and pale furniture.

'What would you like?'

His voice made her jump. He was so tall she had to tilt back her head to look at him.

'A small gin with a lot of orange juice and some ice,'

she said almost brightly, looking round the room while he fixed the drinks. Her eyes took nothing in, her attention was riveted by Alex's easy graceful movements.

He handed her a tall glass, and she almost dropped it as their hands accidentally brushed. He watched her nervousness with blank eyes.

The atmosphere was explosive. Talia felt as though she had a fever burning inside her. She stared hypnotised at the strong muscles of his throat, contracting as he swallowed back his drink.

'Tell me why you've come,' he repeated, his grey eyes holding hers.

'Louise . . . Louise said you asked for me when you were in hospital,' she said quickly, daringly.

'Did she, damn her!' Alex's voice gave nothing away.

'Is it true?'

'I was delirious, my love, how the hell should I know who I asked for?'

'You must know!' Her dark eyes glinted angrily. He was playing games with her. She stared into his lean dark face and her heart turned over. 'You must!'

Alex smiled slightly. 'Is it so important?'

'I'd like to know.' Her fingers played restlessly with the glass.

'Very well—yes, I asked for you.' It was an expressionless statement of fact. 'Is that what you came all this way to hear?' There was a deep bitter mockery in his grey eyes. It hurt her. She turned away feeling utterly depressed, and walked to the open windows.

'What the hell did you expect me to say?' Alex demanded harshly. 'That I wanted to kill you when you didn't come? Goddammit, Talia, it's over. We can't live together, we tear each other apart, and I

don't want Matty growing up in that cold bitter
atmosphere. He shouldn't suffer for our—my mistakes.
It's too late.' The words were torn from him and they
hit her like blows.

He did not want her. He did not care. She had made
this journey only to be hurt and all because she had
been desperate enough to believe Louise and consequently, had forced Alex to lay his cards on the table,
to finally reject her.

She could not stay here, she was achingly
vulnerable, terribly hurt. Without looking at him she
lifted her head and walked towards the door, feeling as
though her skin had been stripped away, leaving every
nerve in her body exposed. She shot along the picture-
lined corridor hoping that she was heading for the
front door.

As she reached it, it swung open and Joanna
Dominic walked in. Talia stared at her, thinking, you
fool, what did you expect, anyway?

Joanna Dominic eyed her back. 'Just leaving?' she
asked with a smug little smile.

Something exploded inside Talia, her desperate
hurt running into sheer anger, sheer jealousy, directed
at the dark beautiful woman in front of her. She let
her eyes run over Joanna Dominic. The other woman
was wearing a sleek fashionable sundress. Her hair was
shining and she was very tanned. She was lovely.
Everything I'm not, Talia thought bitterly. This
woman had ruthlessly destroyed her chance of
happiness, had used the most despicable tactics to get
what she wanted and she had won. It was painfully
obvious that she was staying here with Alex. Yes, she
had won.

'Actually, I wanted a word with you,' Talia smiled,
her eyes ice cold. She might have lost Alex, but Joanna
Dominic was not going to get away scotfree.

'Fire away,' came the smooth reply. 'But you'll have to be quick, darling, I don't have much time.'

'Neither do I,' Talia said coolly. 'There are a couple of questions I'd like you to answer. Firstly, Alex asked for me when he was in hospital—you were supposed to contact me and you didn't, why?'

Joanna Dominic's eyes flickered. She smiled acidly. 'I don't know what you're talking about.'

'You're a liar,' Talia said very calmly. 'I never heard a thing from you. You thought you were so clever, didn't you? Well, it's all out in the open now. How are you going to explain it to Alex, I wonder?' She didn't care that she was lying. She was beyond caring about anything much. All she wanted was some sort of reaction.

Joanna Dominic's face flushed, her eyes suddenly glittering at Talia's contempt.

'Now look——' she began viciously.

'No, you look,' Talia cut in smoothly. 'And listen. My other question concerns the phoney telex that was supposed to come from Alex. Bad news, darling? I wouldn't advise you to try and get in touch with him? You really overreached yourself with that one, didn't you, *darling*!' Her outward calm amazed her. Inside she was shaking, her heart pounding. Outwardly she was in control, because she could see Joanna Dominic's mask slipping, could see the desperate febrile glitter of a spoiled, ruthless woman, who loved a man so much she would go to any lengths to get him.

And at that moment Talia realised that Joanna Dominic hadn't won at all. She had failed. She might be strong, but Alex was infinitely stronger, and that look on her face now told Talia that Alex did not give a damn.

'He doesn't care, does he?' She said quietly, feeling almost sympathetic. She had been so blind!

Joanna Dominic's mouth twisted and she began to swear her hatred at Talia, her control gone. She raised a manicured hand.

Talia stood stock-still, horrified, knowing that the other woman was going to hit her, yet unable to move. The ugliness of the scene terrified her.

Alex's voice was like the cracking of a whip. It froze Joanna Dominic's hand. As Talia turned in surprise to look at him, she saw that he had heard every word of the ugly exchange.

His eyes were hard, icy, his mouth tight, his body taut with fury. He took Talia's arm, his touch incredibly gentle and sure, and propelled her back towards the lounge. She looked up at him to protest, catching her breath as their eyes met.

'Wait for me,' he said softly, and there was a tense urgency in his voice.

'But I. . . .'

'Wait for me, Talia, please.'

The smoky warmth in his eyes made her heart turn over. She nodded, unable to refuse. 'Yes.' He smiled, touching her face, then he was gone, the door shutting noiselessly behind him.

She strolled over to the windows, staring out at the blindingly bright beach. She could hear Alex's voice, hard, clipped, deathly cold, flaying mercilessly, and did not listen. It was too frightening.

Her mind was in a turmoil. In some tiny part of her brain, she had been unwilling to believe that anyone could do what Joanna Dominic had done. Too naïve, that's my trouble, she thought, shaking her head. Joanna Dominic was used to getting what she wanted. She had been spoiled to the point of immorality, that was the most shocking thing. But she had still lost the one man she wanted, and Talia could almost feel sorry for her.

She lit a cigarette and drew on it deeply. She was smoking far too much, she thought, but her nerves were in shreds.

Why had Alex asked her to stay? It was over between them, he had said so himself. What did they have to say to each other? She couldn't bear to be hurt again. On impulse she walked out of the house. She would go back to the hotel, check out and take the first flight. . . . Home? The word rang hollowly. It was Alex's home, not hers. She walked quickly towards the hired car.

Alex caught up with her before she had turned the corner of the house, spinning her round to face him.

'You said you'd wait,' he reminded her, his grey eyes narrowed against the sun.

Talia looked at the powerful brown fingers curled around her arm, and swallowed convulsively.

'I decided not to. I'm going back to my hotel.'

'You're not going anywhere.'

'You're hurting me!'

His grip had tightened bruisingly. He had not even noticed. He was staring down at her small angry face, his eyes very dark.

'I want to hurt you,' he muttered harshly.

Talia frowned, shocked. 'Why?'

Alex laughed humourlessly. 'Take a guess.'

'I don't understand. . . .'

'You never did.'

Without her realising it, he had propelled her towards the beach. They stood at the water's foaming edge, staring into each other's faces, Alex's hand still on her arm as though he feared she would run if he released her.

'I know the full story now. Why did you come, Talia?' he asked in a low voice.

She couldn't meet his eyes. She stared at his wide shoulders, her heart pounding.

'What do you want me to say?' she asked with painful defiance. 'That I wanted to see you? That I wanted to tell you that I knew the telex was a fake? What do you want, Alex, blood?'

Her anger was her only defence against the pain inside her.

'You know damn well what I want,' he said hoarsely, his hand sliding up her arm, the long fingers caressing her throat, the pointed line of her jaw. His touch set her skin on fire and she trembled restlessly.

'Yes!' she flung at him in anguish. 'You want Matty.'

'I want you. I've wanted you ever since that first day I walked into Mark Fitzgerald's office and saw you sitting there.' His huskily-spoken confession jerked her head up.

'No——'

'Oh yes, Talia. I fell in love the moment I saw you. You were so lovely, I couldn't take my eyes off you. I wanted to take it slowly because you were young and you were innocent. You drew me like a flame, I didn't give a damn if I got burnt. The night I came to your flat, I didn't intend us to end up in bed, but I needed you so badly. I wanted to ask you to marry me—but I knew that it was bad in South America, there was a chance I wouldn't come back. It would have been unfair.' His voice was raw with emotion.

Talia looked into his eyes and saw his need, that deep hungry love flaring out of control, and her whole being leapt in joy.

'I don't remember much about the hospital, but God knows, I wanted you there with me. Louise told me you wouldn't come, that it was over. I tried to find you, but you'd left your flat—you'd disappeared off the face of the earth.'

Talia couldn't bear the torment in his eyes. 'I didn't

know you'd been shot. Joanna Dominic came to Mark's office with a telex I thought was from you, calling the whole thing off. I was pregnant and I thought it was all over. She told me you were lovers. I came to your office just after Matty was born, to tell you about him—I saw you holding her. It . . . it seemed to prove everything. I went to France to work, I didn't want to stay in England.' Her voice broke weakly.

Alex sighed, his beautiful mouth very angry. 'That bitch, I could break her bloody neck! There was never anything between us, I swear to you. As far as I was concerned, she was merely an efficient secretary. I took her out a couple of times when I came out of hospital, kissed her a few times, but it meant nothing, nothing at all. She soothed my battered pride—even then I couldn't stop thinking of you.'

'Where is she?' Talia asked worriedly.

'Gone. I told her to take the first plane back. We won't see her again if she knows what's good for her.' He stroked back her hair with gentle fingers, framing her face in his hands, his thumbs caressing her fragile cheekbones. 'I'd given up all hope of finding you when I saw you in that restaurant with Kate. I knew then that I wouldn't let you out of my sight again. I wasn't going to blow it a second time. I found out you were working for Leon and wangled a dinner invitation.'

'You brought Joanna,' she accused, smiling at him, her body aching with happiness as he talked.

Alex shrugged. 'It was a business dinner, she was there to work, and besides, I didn't give a damn who I went with—I was there to see you. I couldn't feel a thing for any other woman, after I'd touched you.' He smiled wryly. 'That night was hell. When I found out you had a child, I was crazy with jealousy. The thought of you bearing another man's child tore me apart, then I found out that Matty was mine—dear God, Talia, I love you.' He bent his dark head and touched his mouth tenderly to her forehead. 'By then, I was desperate. I forced you to marry me—I didn't know what I was doing, I only knew that I couldn't let you go. I thought that once we were married I could teach you to love me, slowly, in your own time.' His mouth twisted ruefully. 'It didn't work out that way. I was hurting you all the time, pushing you, unable to keep my hands off you. You hated me for what I'd done—you wanted your freedom. How could I not give it to you? That afternoon we argued, I drove round all night, thinking. I watched you as you slept, and knew that I had to face up to the fact that you didn't want me. So I came out here. If I'd have stayed, I wouldn't have been able to stop myself taking you.' His voice was rough, she could see the pain shadowing his eyes. 'I couldn't believe it, when I saw you here today. I was thinking about you—I turned round and saw you.'

'Oh, Alex,' she whispered, touching his face, 'I thought you only wanted me for Matty. I thought you would hurt me again if I showed you how I felt.'

'And how do you feel?' he asked huskily, his body very tense.

She looked at him and her mouth went dry. 'I love you,' she admitted softly. 'I love you so much that I think I'd die if you left me again.'

The last word was almost lost as Alex swung her up against the hard strength of his body. His mouth parted hers with a hunger that had her yielding weakly within seconds. He kissed her with a fierce deep possession, a demand that left her clinging to him, matching his passion with a need of her own. She heard him groan as he lifted his head, his breath coming raggedly, his grey eyes glittering.

'Dear God, Talia, I can't tell you how much I love you! We'll never be parted again.'

'Take me to bed.' Her eyes were feverish. 'I want you, so badly.' Alex stared down at her for a second, his eyes burning her, then he lifted her effortlessly into his arms and carried her towards the house.

Talia felt the immense strength in the arms around her, and the knowledge that they had come so close to losing each other made her heart wince with fear, made her wind her arms tightly around his neck.

He carried her to his bedroom, kicking shut the door, and in the cool dimness laid her on the bed.

'You're so beautiful,' he groaned against her throat, his hands deftly removing her blouse. 'Talia, are you sure this is what you want—there will be no going back?'

She stared into the strong lines of his face, into grey eyes dark with a love that had been there for a long time, unrecognised.

'It's what I want,' she smiled gently, touching his smooth skinned shoulders, feeling the muscles tensing beneath her hands. 'More than anything in the world.'

Alex groaned, drawing breath harshly. 'I love you,' he said huskily, and bent his head to kiss her.

The words shivered through her. She had been waiting for ever to hear them. She kissed him back hungrily. It had been well worth the wait.

Harlequin Plus

A WORD ABOUT THE AUTHOR

Patricia Lake was born in Liverpool, England, in 1956. When she finished her schooling, she was unable to find work in fine arts, for which she was educated, so she eventually got a job as a library assistant. It was then that she first began reading Harlequin romances, and three years later, anxious to get out of the rut she was in and start something new, she left Liverpool and moved to the beautiful countryside of Yorkshire.

Within two months after her move she had written her first romance. She was happily astonished when it was accepted by a publisher—especially as it was written, in longhand, in only three weeks! Now she writes at least four books a year, all in longhand – she types them later – from the attic of her house. She takes six weeks off between each book, but when she is writing, she works seven days a week, usually from midday until well into the night.

She lets her characters develop themselves as she writes, but she says mysteriously, "My heroes *are* based on a real person, somebody I've never actually met. I don't think I'll tell you who he is."

HARLEQUIN
PREMIERE AUTHOR EDITIONS

6 top Harlequin authors — 6 of their best books!

1. JANET DAILEY Giant of Mesabi
2. CHARLOTTE LAMB Dark Master
3. ROBERTA LEIGH Heart of the Lion
4. ANNE MATHER Legacy of the Past
5. ANNE WEALE Stowaway
6. VIOLET WINSPEAR The Burning Sands

**Harlequin is proud to offer these 6 exciting romance novels by
6 of our most popular authors. In brand-new beautifully
designed covers, each Harlequin Premiere Author Edition
is a bestselling love story—a contemporary, compelling and
passionate read to remember!**

Available wherever paperback books are sold, or through
Harlequin Reader Service. Simply complete and mail the coupon below.

- -